For Shannon Walters Raftery, whose praise and encouragement gave me the strength and drive to finish this novel.... Thank you....

Ken Turner

THE IRISH ACTOR

AUSTIN MACAULEY
PUBLISHERS LTD.

A CIP catalogue record for this title is available from the British Library.

ISBN 9781786120441 (paperback)
ISBN 9781786120458 (hardback)
ISBN 9781786120465 (E-Book)

www.austinmacauley.com

First Published (2016)
Austin Macauley Publishers Ltd.
25 Canada Square
Canary Wharf
London
E14 5LB

Northern Ireland
1973

Chapter 1

The snug was deadly quiet, as Brendan Flynn stepped in from the usual downpour and ice cold winds, one had grown to expect in Portadown at the beginning of March. He gazed down at the miserable looking, wet Hush Puppies he'd purchased the day before, and hoped the promotions claiming the shoes ability to expel any deluge, were irrefutable and not just a sale's gimmick.

On entering McConville's public house; situated on busy Manderville Street in the town centre. He still felt a wave of nostalgia as he inhaled the aroma of stale beer and cigarette smoke, spiritually drifting upwards towards the gigantic oak beams, which in turn supported the nicotine stained ceilings, all accidentally blending with the horse brasses from a bygone age strategically hanging around the room. And there, in the middle of this centuries old watering hole like any respectable public house in Ireland, stood the resplendent oak bar. The brass foot rails at its base, trying hard to compete with the counter top, proudly glistening from years of spillage.

It always amused Brendan as he walked up to his train of thought, thinking that the oak counter projected the image of years of maintenance with wax and 'elbow grease' and yet, the only care it received was the incessant soakings of Guinness and beer!!

I wonder, he mused, *if anyone had thought of marketing such a product for furniture? It would be okay* he pondered, *just as long as the cat didn't start to lick it!* He smiled openly to himself, about his stupid logic when a familiar voice brought him back to reality.

"Hello there Cathel," said Murphy, the owner of the 'Oasis in The Middle of Chaos' – as Cathel called it, referring to the geographical location of the bar since it was situated in the middle of the sectarian troubles of the last few years.

Rory Murphy still refused to acknowledge Brendan by his acting name and could never understand the problem with using his birth name of Cathel Crumley!

The actor gawked at the ruddy anachronistic face of the landlord. A face with more furrow's than the Mountains of Mourn, his five foot eight stature dwarfed by his massive chest and shoulders; remnants of his wrestling days and subsequent coaching.

"How ya doing mi little Leprechaun," said Brendan reaching to shake the outstretched strong hand that had been extended to him.

"How's the best storyteller and Guinness puller in all of Ireland? – speaking of which, let's be havin' a pint of ya 'Black Gold' and a tot of Jameson's, to start mi plasma flowing!"

Murphy fastidiously pulled down on the porcelain beer pump, incipiently watching the Guinness ooze down the sides of the pint pot. He occasionally removed froth with a wooden spatula as it spewed out of the glass.

He passed the black liquid to Brendan, trying as he might not to reverently gaze upon his famous friend.

As kids growing up in the same village – Portadown – who would have thought his best friend 'Cathel Crumley' would become a movie star. Not just a movie star, but also a renowned singer, after the musical he'd appeared in as the lead actor had become the movie of the decade and a world sensation. Greatly upsetting Richard Burton who had turned down the movie version of the stage play he'd so adeptly starred in on Broadway for more than two years.

The single that 'Decca', the record company had released, which featured Cathel singing the opening track to the movie, had soared to number one on both the English, and American hit parades.

He was always different, thought Murphy; He excelled at rugby due to his innate natural exuberance and sporting ability, with his lack of fear actually frightening kids twice his size, both on and off the playing fields. Born Catholic in a prominent Protestant community, meant his parents were seldom around due to the fact that only Protestants received the majority of employment; in the Linen factories, Axminster carpet mills, Railway yards, or any other occupation that came available. The majority of Catholics were either unemployed or 'Itinerant'.

Cathel's capricious parents had managed to find employment in Belfast; twenty-three miles from Portadown at the Harland and Wolff shipyards, at that time the largest shipbuilders in the world, having some thirty-five thousand workers.

This in spite of the stigma of the *Titanic*, that had been designed and constructed, by Harland and Wolff, and was still a – bone of contention – after years of accusations, blaming the design of the so called water tight compartments for its floundering, and subsequent demise, after the mighty ship hit an iceberg.

Cathel's 'daddy' worked as a labourer, while his 'Ma' became a piece worker, welding and soldering, navigational instrument panels into clusters.

Peace workers were only paid for what they produced, no matter how many hours they worked. His 'Ma' was okay with this arrangement, who felt so blessed to be employed; even though she only received half the pay of her male counterparts doing the same job – upsetting her husband immensely.

Cathel's parents travelled by train to Belfast throughout the night aboard the Sunday Evening Express returning the following Friday evening. Living in between, immersed in squalid conditions.

Most of Cathel's young life was spent with his Grandma, living in her whitewashed stone cottage next to the Shankill cemetery in Lurgan; on the outskirts of Portadown. A place that would become an important part of his life in later years.

Friends automatically came to Cathel, due to his outrageous antics and complete lack of fear to authority. He was seldom alone, and gained from this a sense of power, seeing his school friends, jump to his every beck and call – even the girls! And yet he still felt a void in his life. At sixteen, his boredom with life was firmly seated. His parents were never at home, and the thrills of stealing and vandalism were now beginning to wane. As far as he was concerned, 'Life Sucked'. One weekend his parents invited him to join them in Belfast for the launch of an incredibly large ocean liner, his parents had participated in the construction of, and being completely bored after never finding employment from leaving school, he gladly accepted.

After the launch, his parents decided to go for an invigorating stout and a wee dram at Laverly's bar. This pleased Cathel, who was feeling self-conscious at his adolescent age, tagging along with his ageing 'Da and Ma' on a glorious Sunday afternoon in Belfast.

While walking by himself, Cathel felt like a child gazing into a toyshop window for the first time as he sauntered around Belfast admiring the high buildings and tourist sights that made Portadown appear like a million miles away. The beautiful City Hall in Donegal Square, with its spectacular, doomed roof of Victorian grandeur, seeming to be there to remind the Irish of the dominance of the British Empire.

He came upon Bittles Bar on upper Church Street, its brass plaque, proudly boasting of its past inhabitants; James Joyce, Yeats, Oscar Wilde, George Bernard Shaw, and Bram Stoker. Cathel couldn't help but feel nostalgic, knowing all those famous Irishmen had once walked down the same cobbled street, he was now standing on.

He was also amazed at the masses of people, who seemed to be going nowhere in particular, and yet enjoying the stroll.

After sauntering along Victoria Street with the overflow crowds from the launch, he found himself outside the Ulster Hall on Bedford Street.

"Mi boy, give mi a hand will ya," moaned a man in a brown smock coat, who was attempting to carry an artificial palm tree, of which, the uppermost branches were about to detach themselves.

Cathel ran across the road and steadied the trunk with the older gentleman, and they slowly dragged the monstrosity through the side door of the Ulster Hall.

Cathel looked around in amazement, his eyes trying to adjust to the interior darkness of the room they had just entered.

There in front of him, on a rickety stage, hung a large canvas backdrop of a South Pacific Island, surrounded by dozens of artificial palm trees like the one he was holding.

"Put it down for a second will ya," said the man in the brown smock, who was sweating profusely.

"Get off the stage!" came a booming voice from the darkness.

"We are trying to do a lighting check,"

"I don't give a shit what ya doing," shouted back Cathel, staring madly into the dark abyss of the theatre. "I'm here, helping this old bloke with this fuckin tree, and –

I don't take kindly to some wanker hiding in the dark, telling me what to do!"

The laughter from the control booth echoed around the theatre, as two figures emerged from the darkness, and came down the auditorium towards the stage area.

James Young, the artistic director of the group theatre, and Sam Cree, one of Northern Irelands, most famous living play writes, circled Cathel – both smiling openly. "Have you ever acted son?" asked Young.

"Actors are all queers," answered Cathel, making Young, and Cree, laugh hysterically again.

"What's your name son?" asked Cree.

"Mi name is Cathel Crumley, and stop callin mi son. I'm no bloody relation to ya."

Cree looked down and surveyed the scrawny kid in front of him. "Do you know how long we've been searching for someone like you to play a cocky son of a bitch, in our next production?"

"Well you'd better keep looking," he said, as he eyed both men with trepidation.

The two, eventually sat him down, and after offering him a free lunch, explained, that if they were to employ him – what his life in the theatre would entail.

His interest was aroused, and eventually, they all shook hands, with all three walking back to Laverly's Bar to meet his parents. Cathel was on his way.

His lack of fear in front of audiences, and his ability to become the character he was portraying, was salient – to say the least – and within his first year with the company, had appeared in five productions; apart from becoming the main factotum of the theatre. (His life had done a complete turnaround).

He undauntedly arrived two hours early for 'Curtain Call', at every performance, to enable him to mix with the seasoned actors. He loved the introverted extroverts, acting seemed to attract, and had a compulsive fascination for the 'make-up' ladies, who were always rushing around, creating the effigies of the characters, onto the faces of the actors who were portraying them. But what really boggled his young mind, was the state of undress the female actresses blatantly 'strutted' in the dressing room – they were half naked and nobody cared!!

He also loved the three pounds a week, and free lodgings he also received. Making him, a very happy, contented youth.

Sam Cree, strolled through the dressing room several months later, after a non-eventful, matinee performance of *The Love Nest* and sat beside Cathel, who was busily lathering his face with cold cream to remove his make-up.

Sam smiled at him through the brightly lit mirror.

"It's funny how some audiences get it, and some don't eh Cathel?"

"That's because you wrote the script, with double ententes, and the snobby set, think it's a crime to laugh."

'Thanks," said Sam, inertly smiling. "That's very compassionate of you Cathel. So, anyway… the reason I'm here, is that there's something I urgently need to discuss with you."

"Come on then, speak my lord," mimicked Cathel as he turned to face him.

"Well, I am sure this will blow your mind as it did mine. The point is, you've been offered a place at the 'Royal Academy of Dramatic Arts in London', but not only that, it also includes a grant to pay for all your living expenses can you believe!! It seems some agent or other, visited our theatre to see you perform, and because the academy tries to balance its entries from all walks of life.

They must have thought a scruffy, cocky, Irish kid would be perfect for their roster."

Cathel gasped! His mouth suddenly opened as wide as the 'Caverns of Ballymore'. He grabbed hold of Sam Cree and danced around the room with him. Little did he know he'd just accepted his 'Thirty Pieces of Silver'.

A year later, as a present to himself upon graduation from the academy, he auditioned, and after try-outs, was cast in the title role as a rough and tumble lad, turned rugby star, who falls madly in love with a much older woman.

The movie was to be filmed at Shepperton studios in London.

Not only was the movie an enormous success, it was also the impetus of the studio that insisted he change his name from, Cathel Crumley to Brendan Flynn!!

The reviews for the eighteen-year-old star were remarkable.

Did Marlon Brando just become an Irishman?
Wendy Ing - The Times

What a face Brendan Flynn has… you can spend the whole movie exploring his features.
Peter Bradshaw – The Guardian.

Cathel also had new friends; Peter O'Toole, a fellow Irishman, and Richard Burton, a fiery Welshman. Two actors whom he had met on the back lot at Shepperton, while he himself, was filming *The Sport of Giants*, while O'Toole and Burton were making *Becket*.

'The three men laughed for hours in the dressing room caravans, at Burton dressed as Thomas Beckett, Archbishop of Canterbury, and O'Toole as King Henry II. All three would swig vodka from forty ounce bottles – in between takes – much to the chagrin of O'Toole's director, Peter Glenville.

They became known as the Three Musketeers in all the gossip magazines, and it would take 'Cathel' years to break the vodka habit.

McConville's was now packed to the rafters with Cathel's friends, most of whom he couldn't remember, and the usual hangers on he preferred to forget. By ten o'clock the bar was in full swing, with the occasional rendering of 'Danny Boy' trying to make itself heard over the rabble of voices.

"Com'on ya bloody Leprechaun, let's be havin' some more grog!" shouted Cathel, banging his empty pint pot on the oak bar in front of him.

"Don't ya be getting' me anymore, ya bastard," slurred Kieran McDonagh.

"Mi missis will kill mi if I don't get home soon!"

Cathel placed a firm hand on his friend's shoulder. "Kieran, you and Murphy have been mi only true friends since we schooled together, and now ya telling mi that because of some women ya married, ya not going to have another drink with mi?"

"Listen," slurred Kieran, "I remember when you were married to Elizabeth, ya couldn't wait to get home to see her and ya little pride and joy Patrick, and no matter what I said, nothing would have kept ya here. So don't give mi' ya crap."

"Things change," replied Cathel. "I found out just in time that women keep ya down."

"Bollocks," snarled Kieran. "Elizabeth found out about all the other women you were fuckin, and when she started doin the same, while you were away, which was most of

17

the time I might add. Cathel the superstar couldn't handle it."

Cathel stared back at him through his alcohol induced, bloodshot eyes. "I didn't mind she was fuckin around in mi' absence," growled Cathel, grabbing him by his shirt. "What I didn't like, was that she was fuckin' around with mi' so called best friend! You ya little prick." Blood poured out of Kieran's nose as Cathel's forehead connected, sending Kieran crashing to the hardwood floor of the crowded bar. "And ya thought I didn't know, ya stupid fuck."

Without thought, as he lay prostrate on the sodden floor. Kieran grabbed Cathel's left leg and effortlessly flipped him onto the table behind, sending glasses and ashtrays in all directions. Staggering up off the beer soaked planking, he dived upon Cathel's flagging body and connected with a vicious left hook, followed by his right that incessantly barraged the actor's face. The creaking table beneath them, suddenly collapsing unceremoniously.

Water drenched both men completely, when Murphy suddenly appeared, and proceeded to pour, on top of his brawling 'friends', the contents of a red fire bucket that always hung officiously, on a rusted wall hook in the snug. "And next time, I'll piss on ya' both if ya' don't stop wrecking mi' pub."

Cathel pulled himself up by the brass bar rail, giving Kieran a helping hand as he did so. "Ya' always were a lucky bastard with that left hook of yours," uttered Cathel, as he tenderly wiped the blood off the corner of his mouth with a beer cloth from the bar.

"Lucky," retorted Kieran, "Years ago I'd have seen that head butt coming." Shaking his head in disbelief, he placed his arm around Cathel's neck. "Cathel, mi boy, it's always a pleasure but now I must really be off. So it's goodnight to ya and I'll be seeing ya in the morn." He exited

McConville's and inhaled the bitterly cold night air, the chill, turning his breath into a freezing fog.

An attractive, copiously endowed redhead wearing a tight, low cut blouse; who'd been seated on a side bar stool, walked over to Cathel and solicitously asked, "Excuse me but aren't you Brendan Flynn, the famous movie star?"

Cathel stared at Murphy with a devil-may-care, nonchalant look and Murphy returned the stare. Cathel then turned and smiled into the beautiful emerald green eyes of the sensually attired redhead. He then drooling, transfixed his lustful eyes on her voluptuous breasts.

"Here we go again," sighed Murphy, pulling his tenth pint of Guinness for Cathel.

Chapter 2

Kieran McDonagh walked uneasily down Bridge Street and headed over the river Bann. Turning left at Foundry Road he met the darkness of the night as the rain became a torrent, his sodden overcoat weighing heavily on his shoulders.

Also weighing heavily was the Armilite folding rifle he'd retrieved from its hiding place behind the McConville Pub where he'd stowed it before meeting Cathel and was now beginning to irritate his right armpit, where he'd concealed it under his overcoat.

He was instructed not to drive to his destination just in case British Army Patrols were in the area, and yet he felt more conspicuous dragging his rain soaked body through the storm, carrying a loaded rifle which if apprehended with would net him five years in Crumlin.

"He'll never do it," shouted Joe Doherty – the IRA butcher – as he was commonly referred too, who was seated on the old wobbly steps in the dilapidated barn.

"Ya know how tricky actors can be. Why the hell are we risking our freedom coming here, to persuade this jerk to do something for the love of his country of which he spends very little time in?"

Rory Collins the Provo's Northern Ireland Leader, swung around in the direction of the wooden steps. "My dear Joe, there are things you know, and things ya shouldn't know. But I'll tell ya, if this plan with Brendan Flynn comes off, it will affect the whole outcome for our struggles for independence. So, shut the fuck up."

The rafters of the barn were still echoing from his threat when Kieran slid open the creaking, dilapidated door of the hay loft and stepped inside.

Twelve carbines faced him as his unsightly image walked into the dimly lit, straw strewn structure.

"Where the hell ya been?" shouted Doherty, looking at the bedraggled Kieran. "And where the fuck is Flynn for Christ sakes?" He sloughed over to Kieran. "Look at ya! You've a bloody nose, swollen eyes, and ya smell of booze! We told ya to bring Flynn here, not get fuckin' paralytic with him."

"Fuck you!" exclaimed Kieran, internally trying to decide whether to use his famous 'left' for the second time of the night, or grin directly into his aggressor's face. Instead he withdrew a packet of Embassy's from his inside jacket pocket and placed a cigarette limply between his lips, never once taking his piercing bloodshot eyes off the steaming face of Doherty. "Next time, go ya' self to try and get Cathel on his own to talk."

"Ya mean ya never even talked to him about comin' here…? Jasus!" Doherty stroked the crown of his bald head in frustration.

Kieran spat out his cigarette. "I didn't ask him to come here 'arse hole' because I did na' think it was a good idea." He stood there menacingly looking at Doherty as he expounded on. "Cathel has been good for this country, and good for the brotherhood, and every time he's appeared on television he's had nothin' but praise for the IRA and its struggle's for an independent nation." He stepped closer to Doherty. 'Because of Cathel and people like him, the whole world knows what's happening here, so fuck ya' self Doherty!"

"Mr McDonagh, may I have a word with you," uttered a husky voice that drifted from the shadows. Tommy Corman stepped forward and came towards him.

Kieran suddenly stood with a surprised expression on his face as he recognised Corman's wiry outline and gaunt features. "Oh my god, nice to meet ya at last Yul Brynner," said Kieran, grabbing Corman by the hand, shaking it furiously. Knowing that all Northern Ireland called Corman by his nickname after he and six other escapologists; now known as the Magnificent Seven, had escaped from the prison ship 'Maidstone' moored in the middle of Belfast harbour, and after swimming ashore in the frigid waters had never been apprehended.

"Thank you," smiled Gorman returning Kieran's strong handshake. "At least you know who I am, but I would like to introduce you to a colleague of mine."

Declan Adams the president of Sinn Fein, the political wing of the IRA emerged out of the same shaded area that Corman had appeared from, hardly recognisable with his heavily bearded face and huge horn rimmed glasses.

"Mr McDonagh meet Declan Adams." Kieran froze. It was like he had seen a vision!! There in front of him was a living legend. A man worshipped by hundreds of Irishmen.

Adams grabbed Kieran by his shoulders and hugged him in an affectionate embrace. "Kieran," he said. "I know this is hard to understand, what with your long-time friendship with Cathel. But you have to grasp how important this meeting is for the freedom of Northern Ireland. Tommy and I would never have risked attending this meeting if we had not thought, as you stated, it was not a good idea." He released his hold on Kieran and after a few seconds looked him squarely in the face. "Do you know Kieran that since the English parliament introduced 'Internment Without Trial' two years ago, twenty percent of the adult Catholic male population in Northern Ireland, have been arrested under the so-called 'special Powers'? That means one a day! One a day Kieran, and do you know how those people suffered because of internment without trial? Well I'll tell you how they suffered. You're no doubt aware that myself and Mr Gorman were arrested under this bullshit law! Is that not correct Tommy?"

"That's correct," answered Gorman, lifting up his shirt to show angry red scar tissue on his complete upper torso.

"See that," said Adams leaning forward to whisper in Kieran's ear. "That's compliments of Her Majesty's Government. Not just Her Majesty's Government, but fellow Irishmen! Yes! Fellow Irishmen!" shouted Adams. His booming voice dislodging ancient dust particles that lightly rained down upon the stale atmosphere of the barn. He withdrew slightly from Kieran.

"You see, Tommy and I were interned on the "Maidstone" along with a few other unlucky souls. Can you imagine Kieran, being completely naked on a freezing metal ship with no heat? Being deprived, day after day of food and sleep! They would always come in the middle of the night, their studded boots on the metal decks announcing their arrival. Those damn soldiers accompanied by our Irish brothers 'The Royal Ulster Constabulary' our own policemen! We would be hooded and spread eagled against the cold metal plates of the ships hold, and then systematically beaten. Not in the face though just in case the press asked to see us, but between the legs, or punched in the kidneys, and sometimes – just for fun – we would be jabbed with a cattle prod! Just to wake up our dormant senses. Then all the procedures start again, night, after night, after night, and because we were cold the RUC members would bring in electric stoves and place them on the floor between our extended legs!! Have you ever stood naked for hours with a large electric stove between your legs Kieran and smelt that disgusting aroma of blistering flesh when the penis and scrotum become well and truly fried? Well we have."

He turned and pointed to Corman. "Tommy I'm afraid, was, shall I say, more unfortunate than me because the soldiers said he smelt so bad that they thought he needed a shower. The only problem being was that they inadvertently forgot to inform him that the hot water thermostat was a little 'haphazard', and after five minutes in the shower stall, the warm water increased itself to 'scolding' for the next five minutes…! Hence the scar tissue. And what did Westminster do about our rights? 'Nothing'. We were forgotten people! We were berated and beaten into signing papers, admitting to bank robberies, money laundering, protection rackets, and even worse atrocities which were then released to the British Newspapers and used against us, When I read that the IRA is a criminal organisation made up of gangsters, it makes me sick to my stomach Kieran. The IRA grew out of a genuine struggle from a genuine, oppressed group of people."

Adams wiped the sweat off his brow that was slowly turning into beads of anger. Stroking his bearded chin, he proceeded.

"I don't care how many times they beat me, or how many weird instruments they shove up my arse. I will never stop fighting for an independent Ireland. Protestants come up to me and talk about the bad housing they live in. The poor wages they receive, and the lack of amenities outside of the City, and I think! – Wait a minute! – If both communities are suffering from deprivation? How come the Protestant community go on supporting the Protestants who run the state? And yet they say they are treated so poorly 'Bullshit' The idea that Protestants and Catholics suffer equally is a myth."

The dim lighting in the barn flickered slightly as the storm outside grew into a raging crescendo.

Declan Adams seated himself on a large bail of straw and steadily lifting a shaking bottle of water, placed it to his parched lips and swallowed deeply.

"You see," spoke Adams, his voice more controlled

than before. "We need to keep fighting before Westminster decimates the true Irishman?" He did an about turn to address the whole clandestine gathering. "Gentlemen, look what happened last year! We organised a peaceful parade for the civil rights association that was given permission to proceed by our 'Imperial Masters' in Westminster, and guess what…? Fifteen thousand unarmed Catholics were met by a barricade of British paratroopers who opened fire on unharmed, innocent marches, shooting twenty-six – killing thirteen!"

"Wait a minute will ya," shouted Kieran, waving his arms ferociously in the air. "Ya don't have to convince me Declan. I've been a Provo since mi Gran'da blew himself to pieces making that fertiliser and diesel fuel bomb when I was twelve. But don't try to bullshit mi. Didn't I read where we had snipers hidden near the army barricades and it was actually us, the Provo's, who fired on the paratroopers first, creating mass hysteria? Also I heard from Father Daly that the shithead standing over there was in the middle of the marchers shooting a Smith and Wesson revolver at the army!"

Joe Doherty came rushing over. "I've just had about enough of ya' for one night ya spineless shit! And for ya' information, I was returning fire on those bloody Limeys who were killin' innocent Catholics."

The interior of the cavernous barn fell silent. Adams arose once again.

"So Kieran, why would we fire on the soldiers knowing full well they would retaliate?"

"I've been asking mi self that same question and here's what I came up with," retorted Kieran. "There was a reasonable harmony in Northern Ireland between the Loyalist's and the Unionist's for twenty odd years until that dreaded day in Sixty-Nine when the civil rights march was set upon and disbanded by the 'B' specials. Who as far as most Catholics are concerned were a group of mercenaries dressed as 'Special Police' and when we retaliated against them it became Civil war! I could not believe I was killin' classmates who I grew up with because they were Protestants, and they in turn were killin their Catholic neighbours. It became sheer anarchy until we received new hope from Westminster who disbanded the 'B' specials and brought in the British Army who installed normality and were welcomed as a neutral force."

Kieran licked his lips, coughed, and proceeded.

"After living through the atrocities of the 'B' specials, Northern Ireland felt at peace once again." He tenuously stared back at Adams. "That's why I think we opened fire on the Para's without being provoked. After Bloody Sunday and the killings, hatred once more reared its ugly head and most Catholics started to hate the army more than the 'B' specials because of the killings of innocent marchers, and the black cloud once again hovers over our beautiful country darker than ever before."

"An interesting theory," replied Adams looking rather irate. "But aren't you forgetting something Kieran. You said we had harmony for twenty years! But at what cost? We endure the Orange Day parades through our streets and villages every year. When the Protestants celebrate William of Orange's victory at the Battle of the Boyne. The battle that started the Protestant's ascendancy into Northern Ireland and the decimation of our Irish Chieftains and confiscation of their lands, the real owners of Ireland, and they ram that down our throats, every year! Then we have to tolerate the 'Apprentice Boys March', celebrating the closing of the gates of Derry so's that William could decimate King James's army, also causing the demise of King James II – the Catholic King." He smirked at Kieran.

"In fact I'm amazed they don't have a parade for Oliver Cromwell's 'Plantation of Ulster' when he also confiscated by force all the lands in Northern Ireland from the

Catholics and our Chieftains, which he then used to settle colonists from Britain and Scotland on our sacred lands, and the only qualifications the colonists needed to receive our glorious lands for free, was the understanding that they spoke English and were Protestant. But what of our ancestors? They retreated to the Mountains and the peat bogs, where most of them starved to death and the women and children who survived were sold into slavery to the West Indies!"

Declan Adams was visibly shaken, his calm demeanour diminishing by the second.

"You talk to me about the last twenty years! What about the last three hundred years? Northern Ireland has been, and still is, a one party state. Catholics have always been given the worst houses. Locked out of the best jobs and forever been threatened by the marauding loyalist militia who also rig the political voting system to ensure Catholic votes don't count." Adams inhaled deeply. "Well enough is enough. Last year Idi Amin expelled eighty thousand Asians from Uganda because they were taking over his country! They were running industry. The ports! The Stores! The Banks! They were doing what the English are doing in Northern Ireland! They were taking over! And Amin said 'Enough is Enough'."

He took a deep breath. "The native Indians in Canada and the United States are demanding the return of their land and getting them! Because 'Enough is Enough'. I will never stop fighting the English until our lands are returned to us and we become an independent country. Why Kieran? Because we deserve it, and that's not just my opinion. Senator Edward Kennedy stood before the American Congress last year and stated that the English should pull out of Northern Ireland because in his own words 'It was becoming their Vietnam' and he finished his speech with: 'Leave Ireland to the Irish'!"

Adams walked ruefully towards the barn door depleted

of all emotion and silently nodded to Gorman who then addressed the assembly of men still shocked by Kieran's bigoted, remarks.

"Gentlemen, the meeting is adjourned. You will be contacted. Thank you and goodnight."

Slowly and methodically they dispersed, leaving the barn in discreet pairs at fifteen minute intervals so's not to arouse suspicion. All dramatically disappearing through the thunderous mist.

Kieran was suffering internally, regretting his earlier capricious remarks as he climbed over the moss covered stile and headed down the muddy cart path that straddled the river on the East side of town. Try as he might he couldn't ignite his cigarette and tossed it away in disgust. A pounding headache burrowed itself in his brain; either from alcohol or the head butt he couldn't differentiate. All he knew was that he had to get out of his wet clothes and stash the irritating Armilite rifle.

The heavy rain had almost abated and a steady drizzle transpired, not making his un-quiet demeanour any more bearable. The crack of a twig made Kieran automatically reach for the conveniently concealed knife hidden in his overcoat sleeve. He then swiftly made an about-turn.

"Jasus Joe," sighed Kieran as he saw Doherty three feet behind him. "Ya scared me half to death! What the hell ya doin coming this way. I thought ya' lived near Killycoman?"

It happened so fast he didn't have time to react. The next thing he noticed was Doherty pointing a pistol.

"Drop the fuckin' knife!" snarled Doherty.

He dropped his knife and raised his hands in open display, a sudden trembling encasing his whole being. "Joe, what is this? We are both Provo's!! Jasus Joe, for fuck

28

sake, put the gun down will ya." His voice started to crackle nervously.

"Shut the fuck up!" shouted Doherty, trying hard to be heard over another approaching thunderous storm. "You're a loose cannon McDonagh, and ya' have to go."

"No... no, you've got it all wrong!" Pleaded Kieran. "It was just the booze talking. I'd never do anythin' against the Brotherhood. Please Joe. I've got three bairns to look after apart from my ma, after da had to get removed by the brotherhood to America! Please Joe!" sobbed Kieran, interlocking his hands in front of himself as if in prayer!

"Get on ya' fuckin' knees," said Doherty ramming the pistol's barrel into the mouth of his shaking victim.

Vomit sprayed from Kieran's mouth, covering the pistol and Doherty's overcoat as he was forced to his knees by the pistols barrel.

"You dirty bastard!" barked Doherty examining the vomit on his clothes. "Ya can't even die like a man, and by the way shithead this is a Berretta not a Smith and Wesson."

Grey brain matter and skull fragments, peppered the large oak tree behind Kieran as his depleted body sank into the muddy quagmire beneath him, allowing his blood to slowly disperse with the rain and sludge, as it gradually drained down the slippery slopes towards the blurry lights of Portadown.

Chapter 3

Francis Lynch lay in bed smiling!!

It was a long time since she'd experienced a 'Wet Dream' and she was loving it. At forty-one years of age, they didn't come that often, but this one was a 'Douser'. So, she opened her mind and let it happen.

The man was parting her immense, spread of ginger pubic hair, with the palms of his gentle caressing hands, and slowly, he positioned his head between her quivering thighs and expertly licked her protruding clitoris, sending waves of excitement throughout her aroused body, then Suddenly, and for no apparent reason, she opened her flickering eyelids and peered under the bedclothes.

"Jesus Brendan!" she managed to utter through trembling lips, while trying hard not to succumb to the moment. "You're still at it while I'm asleep!"

His voice drifted upwards like a benign soul from beneath the ruffled bed sheets. "Francie, mi little darling," came the contented reply. "Mi Grandma always told mi to never look a gift horse in the mouth, but surely to God I couldn't resist it. I mean, look at it – it's a work of art?" He lovingly gazed at her vagina. "And what about your beautiful pubics Francie. Why the hell are they forever hidden beneath your underwear? I mean, I know they grow there to protect your gorgeous attributes, but Jasus, why should only a chosen few, ever be allowed to gaze upon them! What a waste."

He pushed the crumpled sheet off his head, and looked up at Francis like a contented cat. "Do ya know Francie, that when I was just parting your incredible minge hairs, I felt like Dr Livingstone must have felt, when he was beating his way through the African bush while searching for the source of the Nile?"

"Oh my God, Brendan," moaned Francis. "I think you've just found it," as he diligently probed her vagina with his finger, making her whole body shake furiously.

"Don't ya come without me!" he screamed, as he quickly slithered up her lubricious form, like a creature from the deep. He kissed her soft tender neck and pulsating lips, as his erect penis slithered like a snake, into her moist, overgrown mound.

Both intertwined thrashing bodies became a tangled mass, as the metal framed double bed creaked and moaned, almost collapsing under the onslaught, and the small swallow she had discreetly tattooed on the inside of her right voluptuous breast, was jiggling wildly as though simulating flight!

She brought tea in china cups, finely decorated with yellow roses around the rims; both vessels looking a little worse for wear after years of hand me downs. She set them down on the antiquated bedside table, and climbing back into the dishevelled bed, passionately smiled.

She passed Brendan one of the cups, precariously balanced on a matching saucer.

He smiled back at her with his puppy dog blue eyes. "Thank you Francie, for an amazing night," he muttered, trying not to spill the brown hot liquid on his naked body.

"You're thanking me?" she answered in a high pitched shrill. "Are you joking? There's me, a forty-one-year-old women, who's hardly had any sleep because a gorgeous, young movie star made love to her, maybe five or six times in one night? A night by the way that she will never forget, and you're thanking me?" She leaned over and gave him a

31

long, passionate kiss, and he reciprocated by exploring her mouth with his tongue until he felt her upper dental palette, then changed directions.

After licking the parts of her anatomy that he'd previously neglected; especially her voluptuous breasts, she suddenly felt his manhood stiffen against her leg.

He smiled, and gyrated his tongue in and out of his slightly parted lips.

"Oh no, you don't!" yelped Francis, jumping out of the remnants of their love nest. "I've got a job to go to Mr Movie Star, and as much as I would love to stay, I can't, and besides, I'd like to end it like this – happiness on both sides. No commitments, no lies, no false promises, just fabulous memories to look back upon."

"But I love ya Francie," said Brendan, trying hard to grab hold of the hem of a rayon housecoat that she'd retrieved from the back of the bathroom door, and was now attempting to fasten the well-worn garment.

"You think you love me, do ya?" grimaced Francis. "What did I say, No lies! Why only last week, I read in the *Photoplay* magazine that you were in an Italian actress's apartment overnight in London, only a fortnight ago. And in the early hours of the morning, Peter Sellers hired a coal merchant to empty six bags of coal into your new Mercedes, which I read, was parked outside the actress's apartment all night with the convertible top down, and the lumps of coal totally destroyed your vehicle's, white leather upholstery! Did you tell her, you loved her? Did you Brendan?"

He laughed. "I'll tell ya this Francie, never piss off Peter Sellers! He may be funny in his films, but in real life. Wow, talk about little man syndrome, and the stupid part about that incident, was that Sophia had no romantic inclinations towards him whatsoever, but he was totally obsessed with her."

Francis looked at him in bewilderment. "Brendan, isn't she married?"

"So what?" he replied.

She shook her head and gazed at him ruefully. "You lead a weird life Mr Flynn."

Breaking from his grasp she headed for the bathroom, slamming the door loudly behind her.

He retrieved the half cup of cold tea he'd discarded and took a sip as he climbed out of bed. He slowly walked over to the huge, mahogany dressing table that seemed oddly out of place in such a small room, and peered into the bevelled edged mirror that hung a little lop sided over the dresser. He gasped. The shock making him impulsively jump back in horror!

"Oh my God! What happened to mi face?" He ran his fingers over his mauve, coloured cheekbone and enlarged brow, methodically working down to his swollen lip. "Look at mi lips Francie! They look like all the actress's lips that I've met in Hollywood!" He sniggered at his little joke which was met with silence.

Francis eventually extradited herself from the bathroom, fully dressed in an attractive, brown, double breasted bolero type jacket with matching pleated skirt. The white bloused ruffles she wore underneath, delicately encroached her feminine neck line. The jacket pocket strategically positioned over her left breast held the double 'A' gold braided insignia that most people in Europe recognised as the Automotive Association logo, where she worked in their high street offices as a front counter consultant.

She placed her slender right leg on the foot stool, at the side of the bedroom door, and running her hands from her foot to her thigh, systematically straightened the black seam on the back of her sheer nylons, then reciprocated with the other leg.

"You know you're beautiful, don't ya?" said Brendan, slowly edging towards her.

"Stop," she said, putting her outstretched hands in front of her. "No more bullshit Brendan." She then abruptly stared at his prodigious appendage!! "And for god's sake cover yourself up will ya? That's the biggest cock I've ever seen, and if you were born with it, you were surely blessed."

"Yes I was," he answered with a smile, "and it could be all yours if ya played your cards right."

She laughed. "You're incorrigible Brendan, incorrigible, but much too much." She gently slid her arms around his waist and kissed his swollen lips. "Tell me," she said, "why is it that last night, in the pub, you had the strongest Irish accent I've heard in a while, and yet today you sound like an Englishman?"

He clasped his arms around her soft buttocks and squeezed longingly. "I know," he said, "I'm like the Jekyll and Hyde thing. I think it's because of all the voice coaches the studio's made me attend over the years, and now I've no idea what the hell's comin out of my mouth.? But I'll tell ya this Francie, every time I get pissed, that bloody Cathel Crumley always seems to rear his ugly, boisterous head."

She smiled at him, and her eyes glistened. "Goodbye Mr Flynn it's been a pleasure, Drop the latch on the door when you leave."

She turned, and opening the door, walked outside humming happily to herself.

The Lily of the Valley perfume she was wearing, lingered behind as she vacated the premises.

Chapter 4

After struggling to pull on his Levi 501's, he attempted to manoeuvre his muscular upper body, into his crumpled white t-shirt, which still felt damp from the previous night's jaunt. He removed his Sherpa jean jacket off the antiquated, iron hot water heating pipes that ran throughout the apartment at floor level, making the building show its age.

Wasn't that nice of Francie, he thought, *to think of drying my jacket.*

He was also pleased with his Hush Puppies, which looked quite normal after their incessant soakings, as he slipped them on his bare feet.

He let himself out of the apartment, and glanced around to try and familiarise himself with the surroundings, not knowing where he was, his memory of the previous night, a complete blur.

The black iron staircase he was standing on, that ran down the side of the stone structure, reminded him of the fire escape at his New York apartment building.

All of a sudden, he recognizing Portmore Street below him, and Realising he was standing on the side of the old Crew's Whisky distillery building.

He started to reminisce back to his childhood, when he would walk past the brewery on his way to school and inhale that unmistakable smell of fermenting apples when Crew's brewed the best cider in Ireland, but alas, long since gone. Now substandard apartments had replaced the copper fermenting vats.

Portmore Street was reasonably busy for a Wednesday

morning, looking as pretty as a picture postcard, noted Cathel, as he observed bottled milk, being delivered door to door by a white coated whistling gentleman, who flicked his cap to everyone he passed. While Hackshaw the butcher could still be seen lugging large sides of beef over his shoulder, all tightly wrapped in muslin cloth, after he'd methodically lifted them out of the back of a battered, green, Morris cargo van, parked at the side of the road. And he was now loudly slamming the meat carcasses down on the counter of his little store.

The brisk march air was now feeling like it could have awakened even the dead, as it clouded the dissipated rain.

Cathel decided to walk the five miles to Lurgan, but after careening along Meadow Lane in the cold morning mist, his body rebelled against his consciousness, and he remembered Robbie Burns' favourite poem 'To a Mouse' and the famous line, 'The best made plans of mice and men', and decided to stop in at Mallone's transport café, and telephone Turners Hire Car Service's to arrange a ride.

Jimmy Mallone, the café's owner loved Cathel. The actor had arrived at his café the previous year, with the most expensive, Gaggia express coffee machine, money could buy; Cathel had purchased the contraption on one of his many travels to Italy, and Mallone just stood aghast, as the machine was carried into his store.

"Cathel!" he screamed. "How the hell can I possibly pay for this?"

Cathel just smiled and gently slapped Mallone on his cheek. "Jimmy, all I ask is that you never serve me shit coffee ever again," and he didn't.

The journey to Lurgan was uneventful with the perfumes of the redolent, green pastures, pleasantly wafting through the vehicle's windows, as the Austin Princess, Vanden Plas, glided along the nostalgic country roads, occasionally blocked with scruffy, wool matted sheep. And only once did the vehicle have to speedily reverse, when a marauding bull, decided to chase the gleaming car.

"God I love Ireland!" exclaimed Cathel as he inhaled the scents once again of the rural moors.

They proceeded through Craigavon, the new town that connected Portadown and Lurgan. Where some bureaucrat or other, ten years before, decided they needed more substandard homes for immigrants, and now the town stood empty like a lesson in stupidity.

"Who would have thought," gasped Cathel, "that the tranquil area we are now driving through is now known as the 'Murder Triangle' due to all the sectarian killings that have occurred here in the last four years."

An effusion of emotion suddenly overshadowed his natural exuberance, as he remembered the phone call he'd received while working on a film set in Turkey. With the voice at the end of the line, informing him that both his parents had been killed when a loyalist sympathizer had thrown a homemade explosive device into the Turf Public House in Lurgan; mostly frequented by Catholics, killing twenty-eight patrons.

To Cathel, it felt so futile, to think that after years of irking a meagre living, his parents had just moved into the old Obin's Manor House that he'd purchased for them as a surprise, and had had it, completely renovated from top to bottom.

He'd loved seeing them exuding happiness for the first time in their troublesome lives after presenting them with their new home.

Who said money can't buy happiness? he thought, as he wiped the tears from his watering eyes.

The hire car abruptly stopped outside the ornate gates of the Shankill graveyard, bringing Cathel back to reality.

After signing for the vehicle, informing the driver to

charge it to his personal account, he tipped the chauffeur twenty pounds – much to his astonishment, and Cathel stepped out of the highly polished, black Austin.

The gates were his pride and joy. Exact copies he had seen and admired surrounding Napoleon's tomb at The 'Les Invalides' in Paris, and similar gold unicorn's peered down from their perches; atop of the gravel-stone support pillars, on either side of the wrought iron gates.

Public outcry had now diminished after he had purchased the cemetery from the Lurgan County Council after his Grandma had died; a year after the success of his third movie.

At first the council were opposed to anyone acquiring the cemetery due to its history, dating back to the sixteenth century. But when he'd arranged to meet with the six-member council for a tour of the facility, they were appalled at the vandalism that had occurred there!! Headstones were decimated and overturned, with tombstones grossly cracking across their centres, exposing, dark rotting holes in the abyss of the graves. Most epitaphs were completely obliterated, and the tangled remnants of blackberry bushes and nettles gorged on the rest.

He suggested to the council, that he would personally pay to have the whole cemetery refurbished and landscaped. The toppled headstones resurrected, and all the walkways and paths resurfaced with black tarmac. His only stipulation being that his Grandma's cottage be moved inside the boundaries of the cemetery, and renovated to house a full time caretaker. His wages being paid by a trust activated by Cathel's lawyers, and that his Grandma's body be exhumed and interred in the graveyard that she loved, even though, burials had been banned there for years. And finally, he would be the registered owner of the land, with any money earned concerning the cemetery project, going directly to the Lurgan County Council.

The council voted unanimously to his proposal, but now a year later the parishioners were in uproar! The gravestones had been power washed, resurrected, and repaired where necessary. The epitaphs had been reground and chiselled by a team of highly qualified stonemason's, with the newly carved distinct inscriptions and dates lavishly depicted in red.

Shiny black tarmac encircled the entire enclosure, with beautiful, emerald green grass, encapsulating every grave, and a brass vase, complemented with a red carnation, stood poised on every receptacle of the dead, being replaced with speedy regularity, at the first sign of wilting.

The only veering that occurred from the original plans, was that now, in the centre of the cemetery, Cathel had erected a small modest home with all 'mod-cons' for himself.

His Grandma's body had been exhumed from St John's – a mile away – in an elaborate ceremony, and her coffin after being cleaned, was transported to her final resting place at the Shankill Cemetery in a hundred and fifty-year-old glass sided hearse, drawn by two frisky white stallions.

It seemed like all Lurgan came out for the burial, but so did the rest of the world.

News crews from far and wide, arrived to film the now famous actor's, Grandma's funeral, and to report on what the local inhabitants called 'The sacrilege and desecration of their cemetery'.

Trouble was, the adverse publicity had the opposite effect that the locals had intended, and instead of sympathy, they received 'Tourists'!!

No one had envisaged the hundreds of visitors who invaded Lurgan to pay their respects to the fallen heroes, who had long since been forgotten since the cemetery had fallen into disrepair.

Remains of decimated Irish Chieftains, from Oliver

Cromwell's 'Scorched Earth Campaign' of the sixteen hundreds. Battle of Boyne Irishman's remains, decimated by William of Orange, in the Sixteen Nineties.

Irish potato famine victims remains. One million, men, women and children, were killed by the potato blight in Sixteen Eighty Six. United Irish rebellion victims remains, murdered in the Seventeen Hundreds.

War of independence, Irish leaders remains, executed by the British in Nineteen Seventeen, and many other eminent souls, all now magnificently resurrected, with 'red epitaphs'.

The first year's donations from visitors totalled thirty thousand pounds, making Cathel a local legend, and also making Lurgan County Council, very happy.

He vehemently pushed open the heavy, black wrought iron gates, and immediately slipped into the weird, transcendental mode he always seemed to feel every time he entered the graveyard.

Passing his Grandma's cottage, which had been refurbished to house the custodian. The first grave he came to was hers. He felt proud every time he gazed upon the magnificent, white Italian marble – remnants from the floor of St Paul's Basilica he'd had shipped from Rome and shaped into a headstone. The chiselled inscription upon it, he'd borrowed from the infamous Oscar Wilde, who had written the epitaph for his sister's headstone when she had died so young, and Cathel thought, so 'appra-pro' for his Grandma.

The headstone read…

Roselee Crumley

1881 – 1965
Age 84 years

Tread lightly she is near
under the snow
Speak gently she can hear
the daisies grow

'Top of the mornin' to ya Rosa," whispered Cathel, as he tiptoed around the grave in mocking respect! He carried on walking up a slight gradient towards his mock Tudor cottage, nestled in the centre of the graveyard. Disturbing as he did so a foraging magpie that flew out of the lush green grass, screeching with annoyance. His next favourite grave, a little further up the lane on his left, was inscribed...

Margorie McCall
Lived once   Died twice

The story of Margorie fascinated him.

It seems Margorie was married to John McCall, when suddenly, after a short illness, she died. The problem was that after her wake, nobody could extract a valuable ring off her finger. Many of the mourners tried but to no avail, and so, it was decided to bury her with the ring, although grave robbing was a common practice in the seventeen hundreds.

After the wake; which is when family members watch over the body for three days, to avoid premature burials. Making sure the person deceased doesn't 'awake' from the dead! Margorie was interned in Shankil Graveyard.

That same night, her body was exhumed by grave robbers who'd heard about the ring conundrum, and after they also tried to force the ring from her finger, one of the robbers produced a knife. The first incision he made on the ring finger unleashed a spurt of blood that released a tornic pressure from Margorie's body, making her 'awake' from her trance-like state!

After frightening the life out of the robbers with her screams, they ran out of the cemetery faster than greyhounds as she climbed out of the coffin and walked home.

Margorie's family were still sat around the fire at home wrecked with grief, when there came a knock at the door, and John her husband said, "If your mother were still alive, I would swear that was her knock." He opened the door and gasped!

There standing in front of him, was his late wife dressed in burial clothes. He fainted immediately.

It is said, Margorie McCall lived an active and full life for some years after the grotesque event, and when she died, she was returned to her original grave hence the epitaph.

Walking on, he suddenly stopped twenty feet from his cottage. His peripheral vision had detected a shadow – an outline of some sort flittering past the inside of the cottage window. It then vanished into the darkened vestibule of his sitting room.

'Jasus, Cathel," he said to himself. "You've got to stop drinkin'!"

He unlocked the front door and entered into the cottage, almost falling over the front step as he did so. The smell of cigarette smoke alerting his senses!! He'd never smoked inside the compact cottage, and now tobacco odour hung in the air like a foreboding cloudburst.

Creeping over to the golden Oscar statue, he'd been awarded two years previous for best actor in the movie *Terror*. He grabbed hold of it by its slender waist and raised it menacingly at shoulder level. He switched on the overhead glass chandelier, when suddenly his red velvet swivel chair creaked, as it turned on its axis.

"Good morning, Mr Flynn," said the bespectacled grey haired man, who spoke in a sedate, English accent. "Did you have a good evening?" He then pulled himself out of the chair – his cavalry Trill trousers, which were immaculately pressed, making a rustling sound against the plush velvet. He looked fifty something. Lean, egotistical, and remarkably fit. He placed both hands, in the side pockets of his tweed sports jacket as he stood.

'Who the fuck are you, and what the hell are ya doing in my fuckin' house?" shouted Cathel provocatively.

"Please Mr Flynn, can we dispense with the vulgarities, and get down to business? There's a good chap!"

"Get down to business!" roared Cathel, shaking the Oscar madly. "I'll smash your fuckin' head in, with my little golden friend here."

The man then slowly withdrew his left hand from his jacket pocket, and pointed a chrome plated revolver at Cathel's head. "Please Mr Flynn, this is not one of your silly movies. Take one step forward, and my little friend here will kill you. Now, please, put the statue down, and take a seat, there's a good chap."

Cathel stared at his adversary, trying to way up his chances, but after a few moments decided to place the statue back on the coffee table. He sloughed into his favourite, rattan peacock chair, bemused by the circumstances he now found himself in with his avuncular visitor.

"Thank you, Mr Flynn," he said, placing his Medusa pocket revolver on the coffee table in front of him. 'That's much more cordial, isn't it? Now, I would like to introduce myself. My name is Major Pedigrew Jennings, and here are my credentials." He reached into his inside jacket pocket, and withdrew a small, black leather wallet, which he handed to Cathel. "Please open it, Mr Flynn, and peruse it at your leisure, and perhaps then, we can relax?

Cathel opened the wallet, and gazed at the photo of the man seated opposite him. The photo was completely embossed with the English Royal Escutcheon, and below the photo image, in black italics was written:

Major Pedigrew Jennings.
Office of Security and Intelligence
M I 5 Security Agency.
Her Majesty's Servant.

A recalcitrant feeling engulfed him, as he remained stupefied. "Can ya' give me one of those cigs, ya' smokin?" said Cathel, throwing the wallet on the table, next to the Oscar.

Pedigrew handed him a cigarette from a gold cigarette case, and leaning over, lit it with a gold Ronson lighter.

"I'm afraid you're in a bit of a pickle old boy," sighed the agent, as he unclasped a black briefcase that he'd retrieved from the floor, behind the red swivel, and withdrew the contents. He spread the documents and a number of photographs onto the coffee table, like someone about to shuffle a deck of cards.

"Well, let's start with this one shall we Mr Flynn, or do you mind if I call you Brendan?" His brown eyes glistening with contemptuous satisfaction.

Cathel, despicably stared back at him, and nonchalantly flicked cigarette ash on his prized, Persian carpet.

The agent cleared his throat. "First Brendan, I would like you to look at this photograph taken in nineteen seventy, of you with a certain Martin Galvin, the American fund raiser for 'Noraid' The Northern Ireland Aid Committee. Supposedly funded to financially help families of Irish Republican prisoners and deceased personal, which no doubt you're aware of."

He removed another photo.

"This one Brendan, is of you again, presenting Galvin a tea chest that held one million pounds' cash! The same tea chest that you personally smuggled into the United States, after receiving the said chest as a gift from Mr Muammar Al Gaddafi. And by the way Brendan, we had to pull an awful lot of diplomatic strings, so's that you and your contraband chest were allowed to bypass American customs after your private jet arrived from Libya on completion of that highly successful banana commercial you filmed there. In fact, I saw it again on TV the other night, and I must admit, it was frightfully good, quite funny really, especially when that monkey steals the banana off your plate!! Anyhow, plodding along."

He reached down for another photo. "Oh yes, this is one of my favourites." He placed his finger on the photograph. "There's you in Greenwich Village last year, with John Lennon, Jerry Rubin, and Abbie Hoffman. Wow, now there's a group of activists if I ever saw one." He skimmed the photograph over to Cathel. "Let's dwell on this one for a moment shall we?" said Pedigrew. "There's you working for the IRA. There's Rubin and Hoffman trying to instil anarchy in the United States, with their Youth International party. Then there's Lennon whose song 'Sunday Bloody Sunday' left no imagination as to whose side he's on! God, no wonder he moved to New York!" mumbled the agent.

"Wait a minute. Wait a minute," he excitedly said. "I think I have a copy." He shuffled a few more papers around the table, and withdrawing one, started to read;

"Well it was Sunday bloody Sunday
When they shot the people there
The cries of thirteen martyrs
Filled the free Derry air
Is there anyone amongst you
Dare to blame it on the kids
Not a soldier boy was bleeding
When they nailed the coffin lid"

Pedigrew paused and sniggered at Cathel. "It's good, isn't it, by jove. I think it's even better than some of that drivel that… what's is name, oh yes, 'Brendan Behan'. The person that you people seem to enjoy. But wait!! Listen to the last verse Brendan.

"Well it's always Bloody Sunday
In the concentration camps
Keep falls roads free forever
From the bloody English hands
Repatriate to Britain
All you who call it home
Leave Ireland to the Irish
Not for England or for Rome"

Pedigrew smiled. "I'm sorry, am I boring you? You seem rather agitated. Anyhow, moving along old chap, here's another photograph showing the four of you backstage at your opening show in New York, and I hear it was so very well received Brendan. Good for you!! So here's a photocopy of a money draft that John Lennon gave to you on the same night, which in turn, you gave to Martin Galvin. Wow! Another million pounds!! I'll give you this Brendan, you certainly know how to raise money." He leaned over and whispered: "Brendan, I shouldn't be telling you this, but stay away from Lennon. I hear the CIA have a large dossier on him, and you know how those people work! It means his life expectancy is a little suspect."

"That's enough!' screamed Cathel jumping out of his chair like a scolded cat. "Where the hell did ya' get all this stuff from you pompous bastard!" He glared at the agent. The veins on his neck standing out like the roots of a fig tree. He attempted to utter another threat, but the stuttering words came out, hardly audible. After pointing his index finger at Pedigrew, he again, tried to weigh up his options.

Cathel himself was remarkably fit, and had kept his six-foot frame in peak condition, and he'd always had a fitness obsession since subscribing to a mail order, *Charles Atlas* course, when he was sixteen. He had reverently adhered to the 'Dynamic Tension' exercises after receiving the monthly courses. Although the clean in 'Thought – Word – and – Deed' that *Charles Atlas* preached, to go hand in hand with his exercise regime, had somehow fallen by the way side when he'd became famous. But the five hundred push up's, and sit up's, he performed daily, were still a priority.

But this man!! This man who had taken the liberty of illegally entering his home. He was different!!

Although older than Cathel, he didn't exhibit an ounce of fat on his entire body. And his cheek bones tautly pressing through his facial skin, reminded him of the granite faces carved on a rock formation. In fact, Cathel deduced, the person at the side of him was arrantly trained to do injury! Cathel breathed deeply, and seating himself, stared rancorously at Pedigrew.

"So tell me Major, you've broken into my house to show me all these photos, for what? To prove that I've helped to provide funds for NORAID, who in turn, help my poor Irish brothers and sisters survive destitution because of all the anarchy that has befallen my beautiful country? Well let me tell you, Major fuckin Pedigrew Jennings. I will never stop supporting the people I love, and the country I love. So shove that up your pompous, British arse!"

Pedigrew smiled and slowly clapped his hands. "Bravo, Mr Flynn, very admirable of you. It feels so good that humanitarians like you still exist, but please, I'd like you to look at this next photograph."

He sifted through the pile on the table and then withdrew an eight by ten, black and white, and passed it to him. Martin Galvin was hugging Whitney Bolger the infamous American gangster, at the side of a swimming pool at the Carlton Hotel in Florida. The hotel's name, clearly visible on the outside of the building. Bobby Flint, Bolger's henchman was standing at the side of the Libyan money chest, after it had been placed on a large sack barrow.

Pedigrew stood and lit another cigarette, then slowly dispensed smoke from his mouth. "To be perfectly frank Brendan, you know, and I know, that Galvin collects the money, who in turn gives it to Bolger, who then purchases and arranges arms shipments such as Armilite rifles, Semtex plastic explosives, ammunition etc, via Belgium, Italy, Yugoslavia and Columbia, and eventually smuggled to your friends in Ireland! i.e. the IRA. And before you start to become irate, or denying any knowledge of such transactions, would you like to see more photographs of yourself with these people Brendan? We already have enough evidence to bring charges against you, with respect to treason against the Crown. But to be quite honest, what worries me about the said tea chest, is that Muammar

Gaddafi donates one million pounds a year to your cause! For what...? I mean, excuse me, but are you people stupid? Don't you realise that 'Mad Dog Gaddafi' is using your political cause to get back at England who revoked diplomatic ties with Libya after joining a sanctions agreement against him with France. And in his deranged psychotic mind, he thinks that if Ireland becomes independent. God help us by the way Brendan if that ever happens, he, being the IRA's largest benefactor, who also allows your ship shod organisation to train in his country. He personally thinks, that he will be granted the right to control all the major shipping lanes that straddle Ireland's coast lines, thus creating a shipping embargo against the British Isles! Well, let me inform you Mr Flynn sir, if your people hate England's dominance now, ha, you ain't seen nothing yet!"

The silence in the room was deathly, and for once in Cathel's life he was visibly speechless.

"Now old boy," said Pedigrew interrupting the silence. "What would you like to do about this grave situation that you find yourself in? We can charge you with conspiracy to commit murder, to run concurrently of course with the high treason charge against you, which will most probably net you forty years of penal servitude, or we could try to strike a bargain?"

"Bargain! What sort of bargain?" said Cathel, leaning over to retrieve another cigarette.

Pedigrew withdrew a notebook from his briefcase and started to write.

Mr Brendan Flynn – alias Cathel Crumley, has agreed to one of her Majesty's agents that upon being approached by any person associated with the IRA organisation about such plots involving himself in any major threat to her Majesty's subjects, will identify such information fully to one of the said agents.

Wherein, Mr Flynn will be treated magnanimously by her Majesty's Government.

Pedigrew passed it to Cathel who read the erratically written note.

"I have no idea what this fuckin' means," said Cathel throwing the piece of paper to the ground. "And if you think that I would ever inform you or your kind about my IRA friends, you are fooling yourself. These are my friends! My people, and we all trust each other implicitly."

"But, what if they learn, Mr Flynn, that you are a paid informant, and these photographs prove that you have been supplying information to us on a regular basis for years."

"Oh really!" he laughed. "And why would I do that for my enemies you stupid man?"

"Because," said Pedigrew. "You are one of us, and you always have been!" He searched through the documents on the table again and withdrew a foolscap sheet with a cancelled cheque stapled to it. "Please read the signature on this cheque for me would you," he said, passing it to Cathel.

The actor looked at the cheque and read the name out loud. "R. A. Butler, Foreign Secretary. "So what?" he replied.

"Well you'll notice that this cheque is a government cheque, and who is it made payable to?"

Brendan looked closely at the cheque and suddenly 'butterflies' erupted inside his stomach as he slowly read: 'The London Royal Academy of Dramatic Arts' and in brackets below: 'Cathel Crumley Account'.

"What the hell does this mean?" exclaimed Cathel

throwing the documents back at Pedigrew.

"Wait, wait, old chap, there's more!" He skimmed another document across the table towards him.

Cathel picked up the photocopied letter and started to read. It was typed on R. A. Butler's, government stationary, with the royal escutcheon – the same as Pedigrew's, blazing out at him above Butler's name and title. It commenced with:

I must thank you once again Lord Ramsey, for interjecting on our behalf to your considerable amount of friends in the film industry. Especially Mr Flanders the head of Shepperton Studios, who graciously allowed us to insert the actor, 'Cathel Crumley' into the lead role of his latest movie The Sport of Giants. Your generosity has not gone unnoticed, and if Her Majesty's Government can be of any assistance in your future endeavours, please do not hesitate to ask.

Yours, R. A. Butler

Cathel rose swiftly, and walked over to the oak, rolled top desk, standing in the corner of the room. Sliding back the roll top, he removed a bottle of Jameson's Whiskey and two glasses, and returning to his chair, poured the gold liquid into both glasses, and raising one to his lips, chugged down the contents while slowly pushing the other glass towards his aggressor.

He lowered his glass and vehemently gazed at Pedigrew. "So what you're trying to tell me, is that my acting life so far has been a sham, and the fame I've achieved had nothin' to do with talent, but was contrived by corrupt officials, and back handing politicians?"

"No, I didn't say that old boy. We helped you achieve

fame so's that you could travel the world without suspicion, and we knew that one day, the IRA would realise what a wonderful asset you would become to them, and that's when they started to use you for money laundering – appealing by the way, to your sense of pride and loyalty, for your country. But of course, we expected that to happen, that's why we created you in the first place, and because of you, we have been able to keep track of all their international connections, and I must admit Brendan, you've far exceeded our greatest expectations! You became an international superstar, meeting and dining with most heads of state, and everyone loves you. That's because you're talented, and very good at what you do, so don't ever doubt yourself. The status you've achieved had nothing to do with us? Shall I say, we just gave you a little shove in the right direction."

"So what did that shit mean, that you wrote in that little love note of yours?"

"I'll try to explain," answered Pedigrew. "Last night, we had an agent who managed to infiltrate a secret meeting, held right here in Portadown, and was attended by the highest echelon of the IRA. You were supposed to have been brought to that said meeting by your friend Kieran McDonagh, and your participation in some sort of plot was to be revealed. Unfortunately, your friend didn't want you involved, and told them so, in no uncertain terms. That's why I think he was murdered."

Cathel jumped up in shock and amazement. "Murdered!" What do ya' mean, ya lyin' bastard? I was with him all last night, and I can assure ya' he was alive and kicking!"

Pedigrew came around the table, and placed his hand on Cathel's shoulder. "I'm sorry to inform you Brendan, but after he left you in the pub, he attended that clandestine meeting at the bottom of Bridge Street and he was found this morning, on a cart path at the side of the river Bann, with most of his head blown away."

The actor sank deep into his chair as tears poured down his cheeks.

Elizabeth
1964

Chapter 5

Elizabeth Rose Harley's excitement was all encompassing, her five foot two slender frame, shivered with anticipation!! While attending Portadown's local technical college, she persuaded a group of friends – much to her father's chagrin – to write and enact, a poignant play about Irish politics. What ensued was a huge metaphor for the sixteen-year-old.

The play was so well received on completion, that the school gym which had been transformed into a makeshift auditorium, to perform the play, could not handle the multitude of patrons who attended the first few opening performances, and after three nights the makeshift theatre was subsequently closed down by the fire department, quoting fire regulation thirty-six! (Something about overcrowding, and lack of adequate, emergency exits.)

Soon after the three performance calamity, Elizabeth and her enthralled friends, decided by an overwhelming 'democratic' vote, to create their own theatre, and after begging, and beguiling every resident of Portadown and surrounding enclaves for donations. The stable loft they purchased on Bridge Street (opposite the College) was now transformed into a sixty seat theatre, complete with all permits required by law, and tonight was 'the night'.

Sam Cree the playwright, who had been informed of the plight of the girls, had not only donated a large sum of money, but also graciously agreed to officiate the opening ceremonies.

Elizabeth attempted to peer through the overlapping space between the lavish, red velvet curtains, that separated the audience from the stage area, and was visibly overcome by the electric atmosphere of the theatregoers, as their voices echoed and permeated, the whole wooden structure of the old building.

She suddenly gasped in horror, covering her mouth with her hands!! There, seated in the front row, next to Sam Cree, was that famous young actor 'Brendan Flynn'!

No, it can't be, she thought, but yes it was. "And he's so handsome," swooned Elizabeth. And to think only weeks before, like some dark premonition, she had visited the local cinema to see *The Sport of Giants*, a movie that every one of her friends were raving about. "This is unbelievable!" she said to herself.

The two-minute warning bell rang loudly throughout the theatre, followed by a mass shuffling of chairs.

Silence befell the auditorium as Sam Cree strolled towards the stage.

"Ladies and gentlemen," said Cree to the hushed crowd, his beautiful baritone voice vibrating off the rustic interior. "Thank you for coming here tonight, making this opening a memorable occasion."

Everyone clapped. He proceeded.

"I mentioned to a friend of mine, how a nondescript group of students through sheer determination, were opening this theatre tonight."

Everyone clapped again.

"Not only did he want to accompany me as my guest, but he also offered a sizable gratuity to support amateur dramatics, because in his own words - these students have shown that anything is attainable, if you just follow your dream!"

Everyone cheered and clapped.

"Ladies and Gentlemen. This person I'm talking about is a shining example of that philosophy. So Ladies and Gentlemen, may I introduce to you, our own new movie star, Brendan Flynn."

Brendan rose from his front row seat, and waved to the standing ovation of hysterical people, his egotism, floating to the surface like a tell-tale oil slick.

After the performance, appearing more like a dress rehearsal than an opening night, with actors missing cues and dropping lines like hot potatoes, Cathel was invited backstage to meet the cast and crew.

They all stood in line, giddy with excitement, as he was systematically introduced to them. He firmly shook hands with the male members of the cast, and gently kissed the back of the hands of the females; trying to imitate the example he'd once seen Michael Cain do, in the movie *Alfie*.

An aloof feeling enshrouded him. A feeling no twenty-year-old from Portadown who was sadly unemployed just a few years earlier, should be feeling.

Last in line was Elizabeth!!

"This Brendan," added the stage manager who'd availed himself for the introductions, "last but not least, is Elizabeth Harley, the delightful bundle of fire, whose boundless energy and determination, created this wonderful venue."

Cathel looked at her in amazement. Natural beauty oozed out of her every glistening pore. She just stood there, elegantly pubescent. Her small perky breasts proudly jutted out of her tight fitting sweater, giving the garment, a perfect feminine form. His eyes glazed over with a mischievous glint, and he smiled.

"Please to meet ya," he said, slightly kissing her hand, with just a graze of his lips. "You were very good Elizabeth."

She smiled back at him feeling utterly self-conscious. "Thank ya', glad ya' could come," she replied, her sparkling, black pearl eyes, burrowing deep into his soul.

The next day, Cathel paced back and forth outside the Technical College like a caged lion! He had just experienced, what felt like the longest night of his life, with the sleepless night, spent drifting in and out of slumber. His thoughts frequently dispersed by the 'Bundle of Fire'.

She eventually emerged through the open, ornate ebony doors of the College, accompanied by two frumpy looking girls. All three, thoroughly engaged in light conversation, chatting and laughing like a pack of hyenas.

Suddenly they recognised him and their conversation and hysterics ceased.

Feeling like a beguiled ten-year-old again, he slowly walked over to the threesome.

"Hello Elizabeth," he said, and after a few seconds of deadly silence, her companions burst into fits of laughter.

Elizabeth pushed and manhandled her friends playfully, who eventually walked away from the two of them, occasionally peering over their shoulders, whispering excitedly as they went.

"Hello ya self,' said Elizabeth. "Don't mind mi friends, they can be really silly at times. So, what brings you here Mr Brendan Flynn?"

He just stood there and stared. *God, I love the way she talks,* mused Cathel. "I wondered if you'd like to go for a coffee or something and maybe talk about the play?"

"I would love ta," answered Elizabeth, as she nervously ran fingers through her unkempt, blonde hair. "But I've got piano lessons at four thirty, and I must be catchin' the next bus home?"

"Well where do ya live?" asked Cathel excitedly. "Perhaps we can talk on the bus."

'Jasus, ya don't have to do that Brendan, I live in

Annachmore, and it's a tidy jaunt from here."

"So what," he replied. "I've nere been on that bus in years, and I would love to go with ya."

The aging bus rattled tenuously on its way down the 828, with Cathel and Elizabeth completely engrossed in each other's conversations, with Cathel explaining to her how he had just finished a 'four week shoot' on a train full of film crew, actors, and equipment, with the entirety of the movie being 'shot' between St Pancras railway station in London, and Minehead station on the East coast, because Flanders from Shepperton Studio's, had offered him the part as road manager, for a new pop group called 'The Beatles' who were making a movie entitled *A Hard Day's Night*.

Elizabeth couldn't believe her ears!! The Beatles were now her favourite group to listen too, with three hit singles on the charts.

Cathel carried on the conversation, making more 'House Points' the more he talked.

"Did ya'know that John Lennon, one of the Beatles, has Irish grandparents who actually lived right here in County Down?" He then went on to explain how he and John had so much in common, that the twosome spent much of their spare time (in between takes) discussing the semantics of Northern Ireland becoming independent, creating a friendship, that he knew, would last a lifetime!

The six miles to Annachmore was rapidly digested by their small talk, and swiftly came to an abrupt end, when the bus driver shouted, "Andress House – next stop."

"Quick, that's me," exclaimed Elizabeth, as she reached for his hand to drag him into the centre aisle, to attain an exit off the bus.

They ran hand in hand, and skipped across the redolent road as they silently passed the prestigious Andress House, with its centuries of nostalgia.

They came upon a large winding driveway, with impressive white marbled lions, situated on red bricked buttresses, on either side of the sloping path. A large brass plaque, embedded in the periphery wall, with its raised gothic letters, announcing 'The Priory' for all to see.

'Well, thank ya' for seeing mi home Brendan," she said, giving his hand a gentle squeeze.

He gave her a surprised look as he read the jutting plaque.

"Don't you be tellin' me that ya' liv here!" he exclaimed.

"Yep, I sure do," she answered. "Is that a problem?"

"A problem," said Brendan, staring at the plaque. "You'll be telling me next I suppose, that ya' 'Da' is bloody Sir Charles Harley, President of the Imperial Grand Orange Lodge?"

"Bloody one of the same," she mockingly replied.

'Jasus Elizabeth," he grunted. "Mi grandfa would turn in his grave, with me just mentioning his name." He then laughed, and held both her hands longingly. "Bloody lovely Elizabeth Harley, I surely have a soft spot for ya, deep inside like I've never felt before." He held her closer. "For a start, I don't give a rat's arse who ya 'Da' is. So would it be asking too much of ya, if I could be seeing you again, before I go out of my mind?"

"I'd like that very much," she spluttered, as her throat started to feel like it was about to envelop like an elevator door. She wrote her telephone number on the back of his return bus ticket and he lovingly kissed her on her lips. He so wanted to hug her but didn't want to push his luck.

She smiled and said a dreamy goodnight, before walking away.

"Yes, yes!" he screamed, as he ran the full length of Andress Road, kicking his heels like a Spanish dancer, after watching Elizabeth's vision, disappearing down the driveway of the Priory.

They devoured each other's company at every opportunity, after the infatuating bus ride. Burning passions inwardly scorching their young loins!

Most outings invariably ended in the rear lane, behind the Priory, with groping hands and long lasing embraces, with every kiss flying off the Richter scale.

Throughout the proceeding weeks, Cathel introduced her to his lifelong friends, Kieran McDonagh and Rory Murphy – whom she liked immediately.

Rory had been appointed assistant manager, at a local bar called 'The McConville' where he'd worked from leaving school.

So most weekend afternoons, Cathel, Elizabeth, and Kieran with his wife, Colleen, (who had become pregnant at sixteen) congregated in the cobbled stoned backyard of the McConville, usually sitting at one of the picnic tables provided by the bar as a concession to families with children, and anyone under the legal drinking age (eighteen) who were not allowed inside licensed drinking premises. The boys used to sit happily drinking at the tables, with the girls merrily chatting and drinking Britvic orange juices, occasionally sharing a pint of Guinness when they thought no one was around to observe.

Cathel was quite amused every time he entered the pub yard, thinking back to when he was ten years old and full of devilment. This was the same yard, that the threesome used to rummage through the outside 'dustbins' searching for cigarette ends that the pub patrons had discarded into the ashtrays on the tables, which were eventually emptied into the outside bins, and after the threesome had stuffed their pockets with their illicit tobacco contraband. They would run down and vault over the cemetery wall at the bottom of

Manderville Street, and once there, would meticulously dissect the cigarette ends and stuff the tobacco contents into their clay pipes. They felt so adult smoking their clay pipes behind the wall.

Nobody even suspected that the three rogues also stole beverages from the shed, in the same yard!

Cathel had spent days, methodically filing new 'teeth' into a key blank, after reading Houdini's life story on escapology, and returned nightly while the landlord was busy serving, so's he could diligently try his key creation into the large, rusty padlock, that secured the shed door.

One night, while manipulating his 'Houdini Special Click' the padlock opened, and many subsequent nights were spent with Rory on lookout, while Kieran and Cathel stealthily entered the shed – their hearts beating like thrashing machines, as they stole only one or two bottles at a time, so's they wouldn't be missed. After reattaching the padlock, they would run to their favourite cemetery wall and guzzle their loot.

Now of course – because of Rory's position at the McConville – this chain of events was never mentioned, especially in front of Rory, who usually joined the drinking fraternity after closing time at three in the afternoon, only to open again at seven, and then punctually close again at eleven, as the drinking laws dictated.

The placable Rory, always adhered to the victualers licensing laws to protect his position as assistant manager, whereas most bars in the area pretended to close at the allotted time, with their 'special customers' hiding in the back rooms until the 'all clear' was sounded. Then they would carry on drinking to the wee hours.

Rory still coached wrestling in his spare time at the local school, and was well respected. Cathel on the other hand worried about Kieran, who had only found odd jobs after finishing his schooling, and was now politically outspoken, blaming his lack of employment, and everyone else's, on Protestant manipulation.

One sunny afternoon, Elizabeth and Cathel nonchalantly walked hand in hand down the old towpath on Newrey Canal way, towards Moonpenny's lock. After completion of the canal in 1742, Portadown was then referred to as 'The Hub of The North'.

The advent of the canal had given Portadown access to the Irish Sea, along with other northern industrial areas, transforming Portadown overnight from a sleepy hamlet, to a bustling town.

Handsome dray horses whinnied and snorted, while towing huge barges laden with an assortment of much needed supplies for industries along the canal. Sadly, the canal and towpath now languished in transient abandonment. Overgrown vegetation gorged off the neglected canal banks. The towpaths now only being used occasionally, by ramblers and lovers alike, its fourteen locks creaking with age.

It was one of those late afternoons that memories reflect on in the cold winter months. June was almost over and how flaming it had been. The day's warmth was now gradually subsiding into a bearable temperature, with the usual heat haze silently vanishing into oblivion on the horizon, leaving the setting sun to violently create an unnatural technicoloured vista on the landscape.

The ruins of the old manor house (remnants of Cromwell's destructive era) stood erect in the glistening shadows like some grotesque figure.

Elizabeth lay on the grassy knoll that surrounded the ruins.

"Lay with me Cathel," she pleaded, arms reaching for him.

They lay together on the knoll, gazing up at the bloodshot sky, tingles of excitement passing through their encapsulated hands, their bodies straining to release pent up emotions of romantic youth!

He leaned over and kissed her. "Aye I love ya so much," he said. Nervously touching her taut breasts, sending shivers throughout her whole being, he slowly slid his trembling hands under her damp armpits, and clumsily unfastened her elasticated brassiere strap, causing her to emit a deep seated sigh.

They made love beneath the glorious sunset, with Cathel entering her with tenderness like his older women co-star in *The Sport of Giants* had perfunctorily taught him in preparation for their sexual screen roles together.

He disengaged from Elizabeth after what seemed like seconds, and she embarrassingly lowered her rolled up dress and blouse, while trying to quickly retrieve her discarded panties.

She then touched his soft lower lip with her fingers. "God, I surely love ya too Cathel," she whispered.

Chapter 6

Sir Charles Harley. Third Baronet, stood stoically at the wooden framed, French windows of the Priory library, contentedly inspecting his emerald green acres that stretched as far as the eye could see, consummated occasionally with majestic, indigenous trees. He absentmindedly as always, stroked his snuff stained moustache, as one would a pampered, French poodle.

Even in his latter years, he still projected an imposing figure of a man – always immaculately dressed, and today was no exception. His Robin red waistcoat that matched his ruddy, facial complexion, was strategically fastened over his neatly pressed check shirt in attempt to hide his rather obese, distended stomach, with the façade failing miserably.

His yellow cravat with its Fox hunting motive, was loosely tied below his goitres looking double chins, and his beige britches protruded baggily, out of the tops of his highly polished, black leather riding boots, relics of his military career as a Colonel in the Green Jacket Regiment.

He never grew to an exceptional height, but standing erect at the side of other six foot men, he appeared taller, due to his weight and overbearing demeanour.

After relinquishing his commission in the armed forces, happily accepted by his fellow officers because of his intolerance to others and his postulating attitude. He entered into the political arena, and became a unionist politician in Northern Ireland, and after seven tumultuous terms in office, his father's death automatically enacted the succession clause, passing the Baronetcy of his father onto

Sir Charles, making him the Third Baron of Dunaburn, and subsequently, was elected to the Senate as Deputy Speaker, with anyone recalcitrant to his office, being repressed with an 'iron fist'.

He had always used intimidation on others who had disagreed with his policies. But this was different!! This was his own daughter!! He grimaced!

She had forever been stubborn, inheriting her worst traits (which were many) from his unquiet, wife's mother 'The Dowager'. He knew deep down inside, that his 'daughter' would have become a son that any father would have been proud to have passed on his dynasty too.

But the cruel chromosomes of life had made his only child, an anachronistic, headstrong girl. Her name was Elizabeth. Not only had she disobeyed him, but she had lied to him, many, many, times!!

He had first heard rumours, about her association with the Catholic actor, from his church minister, who in turn, learned of the liaison from a clergyman in Portadown.

After confronting her with these allegations, she vehemently denied any romantic involvement, saying she had met with him on numerous occasions out of professional courtesy, with him giving advice on theatre symmentics.

He had accepted this plausible explanation, until he'd read that morning's, Rodrick Mann's, syndicated gossip column, in the *Belfast Times*! It had mentioned an interview Mann had had, with Brendan Flynn, the Irish actor who was in Italy, filming a movie, written and directed by Michelangelo Antonioni, about an adolescent matador entitled *Danger in The Sun* (*Pericolo Del Sol*) and during the interview, Mann was surprised to hear Flynn announce that he couldn't wait to get back to his beloved Ireland, because he was missing his girlfriend 'Elizabeth'.

The Senator had plummeted into a tyrannical rage,

almost destroying his entire drawing room, including a pair of matching, fourteenth century Ming-Ping vases, that had always stood proudly on the drawing room mantle in the Priory.

When his rage had subsided somewhat, he contacted the newspaper through unorthodox means, and discovered the article had been written four weeks previous, and the actor in question, was now in transit to Northern Ireland, after an electricians' strike had closed down production of the movie *Pericolo Del Sol*.

It didn't take long, with Sir Charles's contact's, (and the power of money) to commandeer the hire vehicle waiting at the airport for Brendan's arrival, and replacing it with his own government limousine, complete with chauffeur. Who was now conspicuously standing at the terminal, holding a cardboard plaque, inscribed with bold, black lettering that read: BRENDAN FLYNN.

The hollow rap on the moribund, oak panelled doors, of the impressive historical library, brought Sir Charles back to the moment, making him turn to face the tired looking oak.

He unfastened the middle, onyx button, on his taut waistcoat, and withdrew by its fob chain, the Rovada gold pocket watch, that he kept secreted, in the inside lining of the waistcoat. He absorbed the time and smiled, thinking of the retribution that was about to follow.

He omitted, a loud booming "YES?" as he reinserted his watch.

Sir Charles's male secretaries, timid voice answered. "Mr Flynn to see you Sir."

"Show him in," came the bellowing reply.

The tawdry doors creaked open, and in waltzed Cathel, smoking his usual Park Drive, his appearance looking rather bedraggled after his impromptu journey, especially his hair, that gave the impression of complete neglect although it had been expensively coiffured at an exclusive salon in Rome, to give him that 'Shaggy' rebellious look, needed for the matador movie. His Levi jeans were creased beyond recognition and his stained white T-shirt completed the objectionable image. His sock-less sandals slobbed noisily on the polished hardwood floor, as he walked over to greet Sir Charles.

The Senator, smirked inscrutably at Cathel, and pointed to a pair of winged backed, tapestry covered chairs, strategically placed in the corner of the room flanking a gigantic marble fireplace that resembled the entrance to Mausolus's tomb.

"Please be seated," said Sir Charles as he squeezed his ample bulk into one of the fragile chairs.

Cathel followed suite, stretching his long, lumbering legs out in front of him.

The Senator exhaled noisily and spoke. "Well, I hope you had a pleasant journey Brendan! Oh I'm sorry, I hope you don't mind me calling you Brendan, only I feel as if I know you already?"

"That's fine Sir," replied Cathel. "I've been called a lot worse."

Sir Charles looked shocked, and then burst into a bout of laughter. "God, I love a man with a sense of humour," he uttered. After mockingly hanging on to his false response, he leaned over and jokingly slapped Cathel's outstretched leg in a truculent gesture of affection. "Now I know after meeting you Brendan, our little conversation this afternoon will be extremely cordial." He cleared his throat by coughing into his podgy, fisted hand. Then, inhaling deeply he released a cacophonous noise that escaped from his smoked filled lungs.

"Firstly Brendan, I'm not the type of man who 'beats around the bush', so I'll come straight to the point." He coughed once again. "It has come to my attention that you are romantically involved with my daughter Elizabeth, and she with you, which makes for a difficult situation."

He reared up in his chair, and unclasping his chubby hands off his immense girth, discarded the minuscule cigar that had been hanging loosely from his mauve, insipid, lips.

"Let me put it this way, Brendan old chap. You are Catholic, and we are – shall I say – of the other superior religious persuasion. So you see Brendan… it's like oil and water… they don't mix. So what I'm saying is this, the liaison between the two of you must end now, before it gets out of hand."

Cathel withdrew his legs nervously under his winged back chair, and attempted to speak but was loudly interrupted.

"No, no, let me finish boy!" shouted, Sir Charles, reaching for another cigar. "This is not good for your family, and it's most definitely not good for mine." He heaved his substantial bulk out of his chair and stood menacingly over Cathel, with cigar smoke dispersing in every direction. "Now listen my boy. I can't offer you money to stop seeing my daughter, because I hear you make a lucrative living, as an actor. God knows why. So let me offer you advice instead Mr Flynn. Stop seeing her – that's a fucking order!"

Cathel gazed up at him, and, smiling, flicked his cigarette butt into the empty fire grate of Mausolus's tomb. He then stood and confronted the Senator. "Or what Sir?"

"What! I'll tell you what, you fucking smart arse!" snarled Sir Charles, his face getting redder by the second. He smiled back at Cathel, inches from his face. "I hear your parents are happily enjoying the fruits of your labour, and it would be a terrible shame if anything should happen to them in this blessed time of their lives!"

The cold electrified atmosphere in the morbid library suddenly solidified.

"Sir," said Cathel, interrupting, "I had nothing but respect for you, and your position – until today that is. So to get straight to the point, as you put it, I don't take kindly to be taken somewhere by false pretences, even if it was in a firkin limo. You Sir are supposed to be an educated man, but all I've seen so far is a pompous windbag."

Sir Charles scowled.

"I know you are the commander in chief of those disgusting 'B' specials, and I also know that some of the atrocities that keep happening in our beautiful country have been attributed to you Sir, and your loyalist militia, and I shake my head in despair." Cathel was visibly upset. He sighed. "We don't need those loathsome people who lurk in the shadows creating a..." he paused. "Sir you have the power to disband these groups of mercenaries, so please get on with it, because 'Mr Senator' every dog has its day of retribution, and I hear yours is very close at hand! As for your daughter Sir, I surely love her, and I know she loves me. She's told me you'd like her to attend Trinity College to study for a political science degree, and I've no problem with that Sir." He smiled. "Just as long as you're not her tutor."

The penumbra of suspended feelings suddenly erupted, with the Senator grabbing hold of Cathel's dishevelled T-shirt. "Who the fuck do you think you are, you little piece of shit? You have the nerve to address me as though I'm nothing! Well let me tell you 'boy' I don't care how famous you are. To me your life is worth nothing. I can have you snuffed out like a sacrificial candle." He clicked his fingers. "Just like that."

Cathel savagely ripped the senator's hand from his T-shirt and grabbed Sir Charles by his waistcoat, just below his bulging neck line. "Listen Sir," he snarled. "You can threaten me all you like, but when you start threatening mi 'Ma and Pa' who ya don't even know, then I have nothing but contempt for you and your position. And I'll tell ya this to ya face Sir, if anything should happen to my…"

Suddenly irate voices emanated from the outside corridor as the library doors burst open.

"What the fuck is goin on here?" shouted Elizabeth, as she imperceptibly absorbed the scene unfolding in front of her.

"I'll tell ya what's going on," said Cathel, sloughing towards her. "Ya father kidnapped mi at the airport, and had mi brought here to inform me, in no uncertain terms, to stop seeing ya or else."

"So what the fuck did ya tell him Cathel?" screamed Elizabeth.

He gently took hold of her shaking hands while viscerally scouring her madding face. "I told him that I surely love ya, and that I thought that, ya surely loved me?"

She rejected his hands, and turning, gave her father a peremptory stare. "Well that's good then that he loves me, father, means as I'm expecting his bern."

Sir Charles, appeared to have been transformed into an object of petrifaction, 'til he eventually opened his quivering mouth, and omitted a gurgling. "Oh God! No, no!" as he attempted to become menacing towards Elizabeth, then thought better of it.

"Damn you! Damn you girl!" he shouted, while violently pounding his clenched fist, on top of the green leather, inlaid writing desk in front of him.

Elizabeth turned to look at Cathel and smiled as she saw the torrent of tears about to erupt from his glistening eyes.

He touched her trembling lips. "We're goin to be so happy," he said.

"I know," she answered.

They were about to vacate the library, when Cathel addressing the Senator, said, "Well Sir, means as ya goin to

be mi father-in-law, I suppose ya can now call me Cathel."
He then hugged Elizabeth as they left the room.

Chapter 7

Rome, shimmered in the ferid heat, as the wedding party absorbed the aromas and vistas of the Italian city, from the panoramic roof top balcony of the luxurious, Eden Hotel. In the distance, Vatican City glistened in all its Papal, candescent glory, and below the balcony, the 'Spanish Steps', echoed with a multitude of voices, drifting skywards from the throngs of tourist's descending the white marble magnificence, as they excitedly headed towards the Trevi Fountain (La Fontiana Di Trevi) and also the spectacular Coliseum.

What a week it had been!!

Filming had resumed on Michelangelo Antonioni's matador movie, and on hearing of Brendan's good news, had suggested that if wedding bells were in the air, he would gladly pay for all of Brendan's entourage to fly to Rome. He would also reserve the prestigious Eden Hotel, and arrange an early morning civic ceremony, at the legendary registry office situated in the decadent Palazzo Angrafe on the Via Luigi Petrosselli, where all the rich and famous, and anyone who was anyone, chose to have a 'quickie marriage'.

His only stipulation being: no publicity, and definitely no press, fearing that Brendan's appeal as the most eligible bachelor in 'Movie Land' would be compromised if all the single women and star struck marrieds, became aware that Brendan was now married, and that his new movie based on a sizzling romantic novel, about a suave, single matador, would suffer at the box office.

Elizabeth and Cathel's discussion was short and sweet,

both unanimously agreeing to Antonio's proposal. Her father of course refused to attend, also forbidding his wife not too accept the invitation. Whereas the Dowager thought it was the most intriguing thing she'd heard of in years, and couldn't wait to board the plane.

The Air Lingus Airways charter, soared effortlessly through the cloudless, blue sky above the Irish Sea, with the most unlikely wedding party ever to depart Belfast International.

Seamus Crumley and his wife Roisin, sat glued to their seats, with a look of trepidation and fear deeply etched on their worried faces, after never experiencing aviation – the 'Modern Technology' as Seamus referred to it.

The Dowager on the other hand, waded into her second Champagne and orange juice, in as many minutes, while the ever garrulous Elizabeth, sat with her two frumpy friends, Rosemary and Gertrude at the rear of the plane. All three 'clacking' like ravenous hens.

Cathel's only disappointment being, that his best friends were not aboard the plane, even though he'd offered free flights and accommodations to both, including their families and companions. They had both refused! Kieran because his wife Colleen was expecting her second child at any time and was advised not to fly, and Rory, being so protective of his position at McConvilles, also declined, explaining to Cathel in great detail, that to leave unexpectedly would place his job in jeopardy, to which Cathel replied: "Fuck ya job Rory, I'll buy the place for ya." Rory also declined Cathel's second offer.

Through political manipulation and patronage, Antonioni had the three months' probationary period for marriage licences revoked, and had managed to have the registry office, opened and ready for business at six am, (to avoid onlookers). Instead of the usual, nine am start, the Justice of the Peace, who was to officiate the wedding,

74

paced erratically outside the ornate, rococo relieved building in anticipation of the arrival of his famous patrons, especially Antonioni, whom Italy treated like an apotheosis; a second, coming"

Cathel was completely flabbergasted when he stepped from the luxurious Mercedes that had come to an abrupt stop in front of the centuries old, worn down, onyx staircase of the justice building.

There to greet him was Antonioni, wearing the most beautifully tailored, white linen Armani suit, he had ever laid eyes on. The very famine, pink Hemmes silk tie, he wore as an accessory to it, clashed ridiculously with the large red carnation, he had pinned to his hand-stitched, jacket lapel. His long black hair was perfectly slicked back into a bobbing ponytail.

Cathel felt stupidly under dressed in his rented, three-piece mohair; although it did glisten nicely in the morning light. The black leather patent shoes he was wearing, worried him the most! They so reminded him of the tap dancing shoes, Fred Astaire had worn in the movie *Daddy Long Legs*. "Oh well," he said, with a contented sigh.

Adherently rendered, on Antonioni's arm, was the vivacious Claudia Vetti. Cathel's co-star in the matador movie. She was sensually attired in a white transparent, Dior chiffon dress, which did nothing to conceal her red feathered under garments and her voluptuous femininity. Florid, six-inch stiletto heeled shoes, completed the spectacle.

Cathel stood on the marble sidewalk, in a shocked, open handed stance. "Antonioni, I thought you said 'low profile'?"

"Si Senor Brendan," answered Antonioni, pretending to be totally inept at speaking proper English. "This is, as you a say, a 'low profile', you should'a seen me on a Sunday."

Everyone laughed, including the nervous Justice of the

Peace, who now seemed more relaxed.

Antonioni proceeded to pin another enormous, red carnation – like his own – onto Cathel's lapel, and then he kissed him fully on the lips.

Cathel smiled, and shook his head.

He then turned and kissed Claudia on alternate cheeks. Then shaking hands with the magistrate, they all casually strolled through the buildings, monastic vestibule.

Elizabeth entered the musty, aromatic cloister, in the bowels of the building to a standing ovation when she appeared, and instead of wearing a wedding gown – the sign of purity – she had chosen a white, two-piece, woollen Christian Dior dress suit, with emerald green piping around the collar and cuffs to give it a touch of class. She wore a pastel green, silk blouse underneath the jacket, delicately exhibiting the complete ensemble. Two-inch heeled, white lace shoes tinged with green, graced her tiny feet. Nothing showy but nice.

The ceremony was a sedate affair, with the justice activating the proceedings after supplications, by announcing, that everyone in attendance was equal in the eyes of God. No matter what religious persuasion they preferred or practiced. There was no mention of any proselytising, or any priority of denomination, which made Elizabeth wonder about the legality of the whole ceremony, like people she'd heard of, sometimes do, when married in Mexico.

Nobody seemed to mind the magistrate's outspoken words on religion, with the exception of Seamus Crumley, who only the day previous, had been treated to a private visitation to the Vatican, arranged by Antonioni.

After viewing the Michelangelo ceilings in the Sistine Chapel, Seamus was enthralled with the ostentatious gold trappings, and the Godly chastity of St Paul's Basilica, all there in exaltation of the Catholic faith, proudly protected by the royally attired, Papal guards, in their gold and red uniforms, their plumed helmet feathers, reaching skywards to the Heavens – 'The abode of God'.

He now realised what an honour it was to be Catholic, and no matter what religious persecution he'd endured in his country of birth. He now felt the elation that 'Job' must have experienced, as described in the Old Testament after never decrying his faith.

Seamus and Roisin felt truly blessed, but unfortunately on their return to the Eden, they outstayed their welcome at the dinner table by boring the other guests with their exultations, and expletives of the Catholic faith, especially upsetting the Dowager who continually – in between glasses of port – made derogatory remarks throughout the whole religious conversation, making everyone laugh except Seamus.

The intriguing wedding ceremony had only lasted thirty minutes, with the retinue being discreetly whisked away by a fleet of black Mercedes, back to the Eden.

They were greeted by top hatted, white gloved doormen, immaculately dressed in the hotel's green livery, who hastily ushered the diminutive group to the grandeur of the roof garden restaurant, where the most resplendent banquet awaited them, graciously donated by the Eden in exchange for the privilege of hanging the signed photographs of Antonioni and Brendan Flynn, alongside photographs of other famous patrons who also frequented the swanky Eden. But how much food could the Flynn entourage consume on a glorious Sunday morning in Rome?

The celebrations for her wedding soon began to wane for Elizabeth, as the fairy-tale sunset of Rome, ignited the terra cotta roof tops with an incandescent glow.

Celebrities and high profile business types, drifted in and out of the wedding reception throughout the day, omnivorously devouring anything edible in sight.

So much for Antonioni's anonymity warning!

Beautiful people, and the night owls of Rome, had now suddenly started to arrive, transforming their reception into something resembling 'A night at the Oscars' – without cameras of course!

The who's who, of Roman society, television and movie personalities alike, mingled in every 'nook and cranny', trying to pay homage to Antonioni and Cathel, while Elizabeth, feeling completely dejected, morosely sat in the shadows of an alcove with Rosemary and Gertrude. All three being totally ignored, until an Italian actress who Elizabeth recognised from a movie she had seen, shuffled towards them slightly impeded by her tight gold lamie dress, that gave the impression she'd been poured into it.

She shook Elizabeth's hand, and omitted a girlie gurgle. "Ebizabeth Barling," she uttered in broken English, "you a musta feela so a prouda to be a married to a Brendan?"

Elizabeth glared at her. "Why the fuck," she exploded, "would I be proud to be married to Brendan Flynn, when I thought I was marrying fucking Cathel Crumley?"

The actress 'trotted' away with a puzzled expression on her face.

Elizabeth was saddened. She felt she had made a big mistake. This had been her first encounter with the 'Enemy'. The rich and famous and the 'wannabee's', she didn't like them. Women, beautiful women, were hanging onto Cathel's every word, while openly flirting with their sparkling, mascara lined eyes and precocious lips.

"Have they no self-respect!" hissed Elizabeth to her friends. She sat there, seething with anger, trying to understand why she had acceded to this Roman fiasco.

She pined for the normality of life in her beloved

Ireland, but most of all she pined for the man she loved –
Cathel Crumley – not this facsimile called Brendan Flynn!

For the first time that she could remember, she missed
her parents. Okay, her father was brusque, acrimonious,
and at times, an uncontrollable bigot, but at least he had
'breeding'?

Okay, he was born into money, brought up with money.
But surely, manners and respect, like her father exhibited
occasionally, were part of the package.

"Not like this fuckin lot!" she murmured under her
breath.

Northern Ireland
1973

The Present

Chapter 8

Kieran McDonagh's funeral was a disruptive, political, disposition!! Six pallbearers, attired in commando style, black shirt and trousers, along with the symbolic IRA green shoulder sash, brazenly steadied the hand hewed coffin that was precariously balanced on a wooden trek cart, as it slowly ambled through the streets of Lurgan. Their faces discreetly hidden behind black woollen balaclavas.

Colleen held tightly onto the consoling arm of Cathel at the head of the sombre cortege, while bravely solacing her uncontrollable sobbing children, who clung viscerally between them.

Melancholic sadness, overshadowed Protestant and Catholic onlookers alike, as a lone solemn piper, and a methodical drummer, dilatory marched in front of the burial casket, intensifying the maudlin atmosphere by perpetually playing a haunting Irish lament.

Throughout the whole proceedings, British Army personnel, and camouflaged painted Land Rovers, were strategically positioned along the previously devised route to Shankill Cemetery.

A solitary white Ford escort could occasionally be seen, conspicuously speeding across corresponding side streets, in unison to the trek cart. Suddenly, it appeared, fifty yards ahead of the procession, where two neatly dressed young men with closely cropped hair, quickly alighted from the vehicle and attempted to capture on film, the entire retinue of mourners, using their sophisticated camcorders to record every aspect of the funeral cortege.

Minutes later, the cemetery's elaborate wrought iron gates were opened arrantly by two, burly black garmented 'Gentlemen'. The cortege then entered the sleeping graveyard, with the heavy gates rapidly slamming closed once the immediate family and pallbearers had gained entry.

The chaos transpired when Kieran's coffin was slowly lowered into the freshly dug orifice, and like a magician's rabbit, the six pallbearers suddenly appeared, armed with Second World War era, Enfield rifle's, and after positioning themselves around the open grave, stood regimentally rigid. Then, with military precision, cartridges were loaded into the archaic breaches and pointed skywards. They fired in unison, and in rapid succession, ejected the shell casings – using the rifles simple bolt action. Then systematically they repeated the ear shattering procedure in final salute to their fallen comrade.

Land Rovers screeched to a halt outside the cemetery gates like ants on abandoned food, and British Paratroopers stormed the graveyard entrance, with a group of a hundred or more, vehement local citizens close behind.

The regiment's haughty commanding officer, was first to arrive at the gravesite, his army issue pistol, drawn from its brown leather hip holster, but still attached to a khaki lanyard, loosely hanging around his muscular neck. He was closely followed by adept military personnel.

What greeted them was solitude!!

Six discarded rifles lay in the trodden down grass surrounding the grave, with cartridge cases haphazardly dispersed throughout the sorrowful mourners' feet.

Not surprisingly the pallbearers had disappeared, absorbed by the hustling throng of onlookers.

The commanding officer became exceedingly animated. "Stop!" he screamed. The veins in his neck nervously taut, and near to bursting. "Don't anyone move!

Stay where you are!" He scowled at the congregation. "I demand to know who fired these rifles?" He vigorously pointed to the discarded Enfield's.

The congregation stared back at him with impunity, and loudly without restraint, started to sing 'The Lord is My Shepherd I Shall Not Want'. Raucously accompanied by the local contingent of followers.

"Don't you people ever listen?" shouted the officer. "I can have this cemetery locked down, and make all of you present, submit to a paraffin test for gunshot residue."

"That surely sounds like a fuckin' waste of good paraffin to me!" shouted a voice from the crowd – to everyone's amusement.

You could slice the atmosphere with a knife, and realising the situation could become an international incident, because of Brendan Flynn's involvement. The bombastic officer, reluctantly ordered his men to stand down and confiscate the abandoned firearms.

Paratroopers and army personnel strategically withdrew back to their vehicles, accompanied by loud cheers from the hostile crowd.

A small reception of sandwiches, 'drisheen', and puncheons of Guinness, along with the compulsory bottles of Jameson's (added for good measure) awaited the mourners inside Cathel's cottage, situated on the sacred grounds.

Suddenly his home was bursting at the seams with drinking and storytelling, like only the Irish can.

Colleen had just finished saturating Cathel with incessant tears, and slobbering kisses, after he had presented her with ten thousand pounds, and a package of 'Noraid Funds' – to tide her over – bringing heart felt cheers from the gathering.

At the height of the celebration of life, a stranger nestled up to Cathel and whispered in his ear, "I'm sorry to interrupt, but do ya think I could have a word with ya?"

Cathel turned to acknowledge the stranger and couldn't help but snigger. Superficially the man was a mess. He was wearing matted, moleskin trousers, with metal cycle clips clamped around his spindly, cruded ankles. The strained, striped suspenders he wore (supporting the moleskins) dug tautly about his shoulders, accentuating the dirty brown collarless shirt, bunched up around his throat, the frayed collar stud hole blatantly staring out at him, like a deranged Cyclops. The man's hair and beard, appeared to be late for his appointment for delousing!

"Get yourself another drink mi friend and relax," said Cathel, slapping him friendly on the back. "I'll talk to ya later."

He leaned closer to Cathel and whispered, "By the way, my name is Declan Adams."

Cathel opened his lips and released a long subliminal sigh. He gently shoved Adams, obscurely into a side repository room, quietly closing the quaint, stained glass panelled door, behind them.

The two shook hands vigorously, while hardly containing their emotions.

Cathel started to incessantly laugh again after inspecting Adams's outrageous attire. "I'll tell ya this Declan, I think I gave the money to the wrong person, you look more in need of support, than anyone I have ever met."

Adams smiled and placed the empty Piper Export bottle; he'd been drinking from, onto a side table. "Cathel, I haven't much time so let's talk." He ran his fingers through his knotted hair, before folding his arms across his chest in frustration. "Cathel, rumours have been circulating that Kieran was killed by a 'Provo' – one of us, and I'm here to incinerate that theory once and for all." He placed a firm hand on Cathel's shoulder. "As you know, Joe Doherty is one of our most trusted members, and on that fateful night when Kieran was killed, he was making his way home alongside Dermots Brook – roughly the same direction that Kieran took – when halfway up the hill, he observed a British Army patrol apprehend him, and according to Doherty, they must have had prior knowledge of his 'whereabouts' because Joe said, the lead officer of the patrol, walked straight up to Kieran and shot him in the head without uttering a word.

"Joe then waited in hiding, until the patrol had disappeared, before creeping up to where Kieran lay, and seeing that he'd passed on, proceeded to dig out of a large oak tree, majestically standing where Kieran had met his demise, a deformed bullet!!"

Declan opened his clenched fist and dropped a dilapidated slug into Cathel's - outstretched palm. He stared at Cathel and sighed.

"The significance of that bullet in your hand Cathel, is that it came from a Walther PPK super pistol, just recently issued and sanctioned for use, by British Army officers, and secret service personnel. Now, our conjecture is that someone infiltrated our organisation on that fateful night, and finding that Kieran was supposed to have invited you to our little foray, with the sole intention to ask for your assistance in a delicate situation. 'The Mole' unfortunately found out that Kieran disapproved of your participation, and the meeting was suspended." He paused.

"We feel Kieran was murdered because he found out the identity of the so-called 'Mole', who infiltrated our ranks. Which really smells like MI5 involvement more and more each day."

Cathel swigged the last drop of Jameson's from his glass and ambiguously stood eye-to-eye with Adams, his blue eyes clouded with imperceptible conjecture.

"Well tell me Declan, what was your clandestine group going to ask mi to do for ya, because, to be quite honest Declan, I'm beginning to worry about my involvement with the 'Brotherhood'. You know I worship the country that bore me, and I've always been proud to be Catholic, but let's face it, I'm just an ordinary Irishman, who gets lots of money and adulation, to act like I'm someone else."

He lit another Park Drive and blew smoke in Adams direction.

"Listen," he said, "I've gladly helped the organisation to boost Noraid funds for ya, and I know a few things I've done for ya, have been, shall I say, rather naughty, but I've always done it to help Irish Catholics gain equality, and you know I would give ya every penny I own, just to see Ireland gain independence. So please, don't ya dare, ask mi to do anything more than I'm already doin, or I'd have to decline. I think mi best friend Kieran knew that, and that's why he was killed. So let's just leave it at that shall wi?"

Adams effusion of emotion, rose to the surface like a Jekyll and Hyde persona. He spat on the wooden floor in front of Cathel's feet, his mouth drawn tightly at the corners.

"Well, I'm sorry to hear you say that Cathel, because we need you." He sauntered over to the small, bottled bottomed, window of the repository, and stared out at the deserted graveyard. After a few seconds he abruptly turned and faced Cathel. "I'm sorry to tell you this, and don't get me wrong, we really appreciate all you've done for us, but I'm afraid you have no choice in the matter. This is for the salvation of our country, and you'll help us or face the consequences! If you know what I mean."

A smirk spread across Cathel's face. "Well Mr fuckin Adams, I think ya should leave now before you outstay your welcome, and on your way out, just remember the story of the man who killed the hen that laid the golden eggs. He finished with fuckin nothing."

Cathel rancorously watched, as Adam's left the confines of the repository, violently elbowing his way through the madding crowd to the front door of the cottage.

As he left. Cathel observed another bedraggled person leaning on the same door that Adam's exited from.

The stranger stared back at him and raised his glass of beer in mocking salute.

Cathel reciprocated by raising his own empty glass, a look of utter amazement on his face as he recognised Pedigrew!

He couldn't help but smile as Pedigrew emptied the contents of his glass in one 'swig', then giving Cathel another mock salute, exited through the same doorway as Adams.

Chapter 9

The next day, Cathel whistled to himself as he drove the unpretentious, white MG midget sports car, he'd purchased on a whim some months previous. Halfway between Lurgan and Craignon, he felt a nagging apprehension about the daunting statement that Adams had directed against him.

He brought the vehicle to a screeching halt and climbed out. After removing the tonneau cover, concealing the convertible roof top, he discarding it underneath the miniscule rear seat and proceeded to erect the black canvas foldaway roof, making sure to clamp it securely onto the windshield surround.

He climbed back into the sports car, contentedly thinking that President Kennedy would still be alive, if only he'd kept the convertible roof closed on his Lincoln that day in Dallas.

He speedily drove down the winding driveway protected by the marble lions, and his abrupt stop, at the rear entrance of the 'Priory', was accompanied by the crushing sound of the gravel beneath the vehicle's Dunlop tires. He blasted the cars horn to announce his arrival, not only to alert his son Patrick, but also to annoy Sir Charles, who hated him immensely.

The 'Priory' was the only home Patrick had known for the last six years, since his parent's marriage had ended in divorce. Their first two years together had been a tumultuous affair after the 'Roman Fiasco'.

Elizabeth had returned to Ireland the day after her

incipient wedding, accompanied by her Irish contingent, while Cathel remained behind to resume filming *The Danger in the Sun* incessantly flying back and forth to Belfast to see his wife 'Elizabeth' whenever the movie's schedule would allow.

These were precious moments for Elizabeth to indulge herself lovingly, on 'Cathel Crumley'. The days and months spent with Cathel (in between movies) were the happiest she had ever been in her adult life. But alas, the days and months that he was away, were her darkest. She still hated the adulation her husband received, every time they left the confines of their rented cottage, and became violently irate at times, bigotry shouting "Fuck off" to anyone who disturbed their romantic interludes, especially in restaurants. Cathel politely explained her behaviour on 'Prenatal Depression'.

Every one of Cathel's departure days were met with hours of tears before she eventually 'packed her bags' to stay at the Priory in his absence.

The Senator would seize these opportunities, while she was living 'under his roof' to venomously berate her about the disgusting choices she had made in her life – and then, if by magic, he always seemed to produce gossip magazines from around the world, showing photos of Brendan Flynn –her husband – frequenting nightclubs, and attending lavish parties, in various locations throughout Rome, invariably accompanied by beautiful and voluptuous women.

Her pregnant state rapidly developed, with an intensity of outrageous depressions.

Baby Patrick arrived the following March, bringing unity and happiness, to the Crumley household, with the loving couple worshipping their child unconditionally, and once again their Friday nights, and Sunday afternoons were spent with their true friends at the McConville –

unmolested.

A drastic change manifested itself over Sir Charles, who adoringly treated his grandchild Patrick, like the son he never had, incessantly talking about the nannies he should be raised by. The private schools his name should be registered with when he became old enough to attend, etc, etc, etc. Much to the chagrin of Cathel.

His sabbaticals from movies, and personal appearances became less frequent, with Elizabeth refusing to accompany him on anything pertaining to his profession. Calling his so-called movie friends 'Plastic and Pretentious'.

Elizabeth found herself, spending most of her 'alone time' with Cathel's real friends in Ireland, especially Keiran who continued to shower her with kindness and devotion. The calamity came on Patrick's second birthday being celebrated at the Priory.

The whole family were seated around the twelve seat, oak table, situated in the baroque dining room. Patrick blew out the candles on the ridiculously decorated birthday cake, and the Senator stepped forward and presented Elizabeth with a gift wrapped package, held together with a silk, red ribbon.

Everyone smiled with anticipation – even Sir Charles! Until she pulled at the bow in the centre of the ribbon, and the package silently opened, revealing a copy of the March edition of *Photoplay* that ceremoniously slid across the highly polished table.

The headlines on the glossy front cover, blatantly glared out at everyone!

'ACTRESS PREGNANT WITH BRENDAN FLYNN'S CHILD'.

The look of shock and astonishment, engulfed the whole room, with Elizabeth climatically screaming, "BASTARD!" at the top of her bloated lungs, followed by a disruptive exit from the proceedings.

A year later she was accepted by Trinity College, Dublin, as a four-year political science student, but was expelled in her sophomore year, when she was charged with inciting a riot, after walking in front of a crowd of protesters through Bogside, with a megaphone to her lips, denouncing and condemning, the Catholic civil rights marches that were taking place throughout Northern Ireland.

The 'Fire and Brimstone' reverend – the Right Honourable Reverend Ian Paisley, who was forever receiving adverse publicity for his bombastic attitude towards the Roman Catholic Faith – especially after referring to the Pope as the 'Antichrist heard about Elizabeth's antics and political passions, and arranged to meet with her.

He explained to her at their first meeting, that he was disillusioned and disappointed with the UUP – The Ulster Unionist Party – of which her father was a prominent member, and because of their archaic beliefs, he was about to form a new party called the DUP – The Democratic Unionist Party – and would she like to join him as a candidate and co-spokesperson.

She was delighted.

In nineteen seventy-two, most of the hardliners of the Ulster Unionist separated, and supported Elizabeth and Ian Paisley. Six months later, she stood against the 'Irish Republican Socialist Party' candidate, and unanimously outvoted him, becoming the second youngest women MP to be seated in Westminster. Her father resigned from the UUP to stand by her.

The ivory coloured entrance door with its brass lion's head knocker, flew open and Patrick bounded out gregariously, and leapt into his father's arms. He was tall and skinny for his age, his grey flannelled school uniform with its short trousers and knee length woollen stockings, exaggerating the length of his spindly legs.

"Father!" he shouted, as he held tightly to Cathel's shoulders. "I've missed you."

His father kissed him gently on his forehead. Then releasing Patrick's grasp, lowered him down to the gravel path. "I've surely missed ya too," he said, "and look at ya, I think you've grown since the last time I saw ya."

"Father," he replied, "you only saw me a month ago."

"Really, well I guess then, it must surely be the food they're givin ya here, and speaking of who's givin' what to who Patrick, where's that Member of Parliament mother of yours?" Cathel sniggered and hugged him once again with repeated affection.

Patrick broke away and Cathel chased him through the intricate, quarry stone archway, guarded by the medieval grotesque Gargoyles menacingly peering down from the roofs ramparts.

They ran down the inner sanctum of the house and ascended the steep inside staircase, with its carved balustrades, and well-trodden, floral Axminster stair carpet that deadened their rapid ascent.

Elizabeth arose from behind her writing desk, smiling joyously as they entered her elegant, upstairs suite, with its centuries old tapestry curtains and ornate Regency chairs – their bases tastefully covered in French chintz that matched the heavily embossed, brocade wallpaper that lined most of the walls.

"Hello there Mr Flynn," she said.

"Hello there to you too, your Ladyship," came his reply, in his best, English accent. He then kissed the back of her hand as usual.

"Mother," father seems to think that I have grown some, since the last time he saw me."

"Yes, I suppose he does darling," she said, with a hint of sarcasm seeping into her voice. She seated herself at her desk, and lit a cigarette that she removed from a large, silver cigarette box in front of her.

Patrick walked over and politely addressed Cathel. "I'm so sorry I cannot stay father, and I do sincerely apologise, but grandfar is taking me for a little canter on my new horse. Also father," he excitedly said, "Grandfar says that if I keep riding as good as I have been, I will soon be ready for jumping gates." At that, he ran from the room leaving Cathel in total disbelief.

He sat down in front of Elizabeth's rosewood writing desk, and with both palms facing upwards, stared at her. "Elizabeth," he sighed. "I really don't believe you're bringing our son up to respect me. I mean, it seems like every time I talk to him I feel like I should be addressing him as 'Sir'."

She laughed loudly and reached over and stroked the back of his hands. "Cathel, we made a wonderful son, and one day if my Da has is way, he will eventually be running a united Ireland."

Now it was Cathel's turn to laugh. "Jasus, I hope I'm around to see that miracle."

She tightly kept hold of his hands, her watering red rimmed eyes, exposing her false composure. She stammered. "I am so sorry I didn't make it to Kieran's funeral Cathel." Drawing a deep breath, she said, "You know I loved him dearly but as you can imagine circumstances prevailed, and it wouldn't have been politically correct of me to have been seen there, and I'm sure his IRA friends would not have been pleased to have seen me there also." She turned her head, as a tear rolled down her left cheek.

Cathel rose from his chair, and attempted to walk around the desk to hug her. She venomously held up her hands and stopped him.

"No. Please Cathel, don't piss me off. Every time I show some sort of emotion you think it's your god given right to comfort me, well I'm sorry, you lost that fuckin right a long time ago."

"Oh, I'm sorry your Ladyship," he exclaimed. He responded by slowly retreating to the door, where he gave a sort of Walter Raleigh royal bow. He then blew a kiss in Elizabeth's direction. "One day your ladyship, you'll come grovelling on your knees for my lovin'."

His screeching laughter echoed down the upstairs hallway, in response to her throwing a large, heavy black stapler as he rapidly closed the door.

She shook her head in wonderment as an acquiescent smile broadened her face.

Cathel briskly vaulted down the elegant staircase, looking up as he did so at the imposing portrait of the first Baronet of Dunaburn hanging majestically on the facing wall of the stairwell, its gilt Chippendale frame radiating craftsmanship of days past.

He grimaced and clenched his fist at the painting. "You're the Lummox that started all this shit," he shouted.

He stopped and gazed up at the Baron, who was stately attired in all his finery, while posing for the artist. He exhibited the same contemptuous scowl that had been passed down through the generations. He gave the painting the two fingered salute, and exited the Manor house still reminiscing about Elizabeth as he strolled across the driveway towards his sports car.

"God, she looked ravishing," he said to himself.

She was self-assured – curves in the right places, and well, just fuckin gorgeous.

"Jasus did I fuck up," he muttered to himself.

He thought about all the beautiful women he had made love too, famous wonderful women from all walks of life. Women whom any hot blooded male would have given their 'right arm' just to have had a conversation with, and yet, every time he had made love to any of them and reached a climax, this overwhelming feeling came over him to leave – vacate the premises – no small talk – no kissing – no words of endearment – nothing – he just wanted to leave – immediately.

THAT'S WHEN HE MISSED ELIZABETH.

When they had made love, they became one, neither wanting to let go. They would whisper words of love to each other 'til they eventually fell asleep, their sexual appendages lovingly entwined, waking the next morning still attached!!

Why did other women, not affect him that way?

Except of course 'Francis'. Now she was different! She was a Multi Orgasm Gusher? Her first orgasm with him was as if the flood gates of hell had opened, and ten minutes later, he couldn't resist trying it again to see if it had been a 'fluke', but there it was again!! So on the third try, he lay underneath her naked body, and using his fingers and lips, waited for the torrent, and out it came, saturating his whole being.

"Wow!" he shouted. It wasn't love but it certainly kept him there for the night, even though he was shrouded in the sodden sheets that smelt like 'New Morn Hay' – he loved the aroma!

He made a mental note to himself: Telephone the Automobile Association offices tomorrow and ask for Fran.

He started to whistle as he drove away from the Priory.

Chapter 10

The little sports car jauntily drove along the narrow back lanes heading towards Newcastle; the seaside resort on the east coast of Northern Ireland. Its side windows rolled open, to enable Cathel to inhale the fragrances of the delightful morning.

He had made the appointment for noon, giving himself plenty of time to reach his destination, after arranging to meet the Minister of Tourism Gary Fit, even though the phone call he'd received was short and sweet, with the Minister politely asking Cathel, if he would mind participating in a tourist video being filmed along the five miles of golden sands of Newcastle.

This had given him 'food for thought'.

How could they promote Northern Ireland as a tourist haven with all the troubles escalating? But what the hell, he thought, so he arranged to meet the Minister anyway.

An hour later, after rounding the bend opposite Randle's farm; where years ago farmer Randle had made amazing vodka out of fermented potatoes. That is, until the authorities found out.

He suddenly slammed on the brakes! There in front of him, was a desultory herd of cows blocking the road. His face started to twitch, as he noticed in his rear view mirror, a maroon Humber super snipe, appearing from nowhere, and screeching to a halt behind his vehicle.

Three heavily armed 'Libyans' jumped out from the Humber and surrounded his car.

Swiftly, one reached in through the open window and

switched off the ignition, withdrawing the keys in one fluid motion, giving Cathel little time to react.

The taller of the three who seemed to be in charge, shouted a command in Arabic, then wrenching open the MG's left door, menacingly pointed a FN-FAL battle rifle at Cathel's head.

Cathel stared at him and nonchalantly lit a cigarette.

"Good morning Mr Flynn," said the man in broken English. "It is pleasure to meet you." He smiled showing an immaculate set of gold filled teeth. "I have seen many your movies, in Anglice dubbed, yes."

Cathel laughed. "Well mi friend, if it's an autographed photo you're after, all ya had to do was ask."

"You funny man Mr Flynn, now please, move out the car."

"Certainly," he answered. "I'll gladly move the car if you'd give me back my keys."

The mercenary gave him a vicious look. "You try to be too funny Mr Flynn, now move self from car. Now!"

"Well, why didn't you say so?" replied Cathel, gingerly extracting himself from the vehicle. He stood with his arms folded, trying to project an arrogance of impunity as he mentally redressed his captors. He couldn't help but make a comparison between the three men who'd apprehended him, to military personnel he'd been introduced too while filming the banana commercial in Libya. They all possessed the same, mahogany saddened eyes. The same depressed eyes that had mesmerised him years ago, after once seeing the famous gorilla 'Guy' at the London Zoo. His eyes also had that sorrowful intensity: searching, absorbing and menacing.

He was hustled into the rear seating area of the Humber, the smell of garlic and mildewed leather engulfing him from the interior, where he was roughly blindfolded with a black cloth hood, also emitting a disgusting, pungent odour.

The fourth member of the 'snatch squad'; the driver of the Humber, swiftly jumped into the driver's seat of the M.G. and maliciously reversed Cathel's sports car through the abandoned farmyard entrance, ramming it into first gear with a deafening grind of the clutch plates, before driving out of the yard and down the lane in the direction that Cathel had approached from, with the Humber doing likewise.

The cumbersome Super Snipe, with its chattering Perkins four diesel engine, ambled along the picturesque country lanes with its three abductees talking fast and furious between themselves, in Arabic.

"Ay you lot!" shouted Cathel, who was squashed between two of the Libyans on the rear bench seat. "Can ya speak English so's I can listen to what the hell you're sayin?"

The FN-FAL rifle butt connected with Cathel's sternum, knocking the 'pompous' wind out of his sails.

"Well, that surely was not very nice of yus," panted Cathel, gasping furiously for breath.

They drove on for a few more miles, when suddenly the vehicle bumped and creaked as it left the desolate lane, bouncing haphazardly on its rusted leaf springs as it navigated an uneven cart path, with the Humber finishing its jaunt inside a parched, wooden barn situated in the centre of some sort of dairy farm. The odour of animal fodder and poultry droppings, permeating the closeted structure.

After being dragged upon stone steps and through doorways, he was manually deposited on a dilapidated armchair, its broken supports much to be desired.

The cloth hood was violently ripped away, and he rubbed his eyes to clear his blurred vision.

There, seated in front of him was Declan Adams and Rory Collins.

"Well Cathel, how was your trip?" said Adams.

"Go fuck yourself!' he exclaimed, as he gazed around the interior of the building, trying to familiarise himself to his whereabouts. "Were ya lonely up here or something Declan and in need of company?"

Adams made a loud retort by stamping his military style boots on the wooden floorboards when he stood. "Well Cathel, I'm sorry we had to resort to these tactics, but time is of the essence, and after our last meeting, and the derogatory remarks you directed towards me, I realised something drastic had to be activated and here you are."

Cathel shuffled uneasily in the moth eaten chair.

"Firstly Cathel, I'd like to introduce you to the gentleman on your left, who I think you've already met."

"Really?" said Cathel. "And why would you be thinking that?"

Adams snuffled and carried on with the introductions. "The taller of these two gentlemen, with the scruffy beard and the ugly scar on his left cheek, is General Melud Ali Yahmed."

The General bowed.

"Next to him. The one with the impressive, upper body is Major Salah Dun Halasa. Both these gentlemen are members of the Mukhabarat Secret Service Police, who have been training our Provo's for the last year in a small town in Libya called Bani Walid, and by the way, these officers are both experts in guerrilla warfare and explosive detonation, and have been kindly loaned to us by our good friend and benefactor, Muamar Gaddafi."

"What's he doing, covering his bets?" retorted Cathel.

Declan frowned. "Oh, and I forgot to mention Cathel, General Yahmed has a wicked sense of humour, but I'm afraid he also has a passion for killing people in macabre, and disgusting ways."

The General smiled.

"Well, arn't you a nice fella," uttered Cathel, as he stared morosely at the General.

Adams lit two cigarettes and passed one over to Cathel. "So let's begin, shall we?" He proceeded by blowing a perfect smoke ring from his mouth. "It came to our attention a few months ago, that you Mr Brendan Flynn, had agreed to sing at a concert in August, arranged by the British Forces Entertainment Foundation. Along with the Irish folk group Tin Lizzy, who, by the way, are riding high on the charts with their hit record – Whiskey in a Jar – but for the life of me, I can't see what all the fuss is about, I mean, look at those kids and their way of dress, it's disgusting. Also I hear that Horslips, who I do like, are also appearing with you. Quite an impressive ensemble, eh Cathel. Anyhow the point of all this, is that we've been informed that a rough estimate of attendance at this 'shindig' being held at the Thiepval Barracks, at the Officers Mess theatre there, will be 'five thousand!' Not just five thousand, Cathel, but five thousand, British Army Personnel!"

Cathel insipidly looked at the two men seated in front of him, their intentions suddenly becoming perfectly clear. He wiped the sweat from his upper lip with his thumb and fore finger. "Wait?" he said. "Don't you two be telling me anymore, because if you two fucks are planning to do something on that night, you're out of your fuckin' minds!"

Declan's whole body seemed to shake with an exaggerated tremor as he spoke. "Just think Cathel, just think. If we can pull this off, and potentially assassinate a few thousand British Army bastards in one fell swoop, Westminster would have to reconsider their foreign policy with regards to Northern Ireland. Public opinion will be completely against them because of all the deaths being incurred fighting us."

He inhaled more tobacco smoke the more excited he became.

"Look what happened in America last year, when public opinion went against the American government, with regards to Vietnam, they had to withdraw their forces. And what happened Cathel?" He smiled. "I'll tell you what happened – the Vietnamese took back their country."

Cathel stroked the stubble on his chin in disbelief. "Are you two stupid? You won't get within five miles of the concert."

"Ah, that's where you're wrong Cathel, we already have a fool proof plan, thanks to General Yahmed here and his expertise."

The General again smiled.

Cathel looked up at the leering General and then back at Adams. "Declan, do you mind if we get rid of this laughing hyena for a few minutes while we talk."

Adams withdrew a Webley pistol from his coat pocket, and cocking the pistols trigger loaded the chamber, before placing the pistol on the wooden floor at the side of his chair. "Just a precaution Cathel," he said. "Gentlemen, could you please wait outside for a few moments."

The Libyans politely agreed, and on their way out the General patted Cathel on the top of his head.

"Now you be's a good boy, you hears."

"Yes Da," replied Cathel as he frustratedly dispersed tobacco smoke throughout the dilapidated room.

The Libyans departed, and Cathel stood and stretched his legs, as he stared at Adams and Collins with a sorrowful demise.

"Well I hope you've seriously thought this through, because if anything goes wrong with your ridiculous concert idea, the IRA would lose all the respect it's gained in the last thirty years." He discarded his cigarette. "Now gentlemen, I've something else for ya to chew on." He lit another Park Drive. "Two months ago, while in New York I was invited by Senator Edward Kennedy –our long-time supporter, to attend a cocktail party at the Rockefeller Centre, and during the course of the evening, he introduc ed me to John Delorean, an executive of General Motors who achieved notoriety for his designs of the GTO muscle car and the two seat Firebird, which I'm sure you know made millions for GM."

"Yes, yes. So what!" screamed Adams.

Cathel proceeded. "Mr Delorean pulled me to one side and told me that Senator Kennedy thought his new project might interest the IRA."

Adams sniggered openly, and loudly whispered to Collins, "Well that was considerate of him, eh Rory?"

"Listen will ya!" said Cathel. "He told me he'd designed a new concept two seater, all aluminium bodied sports car, and he was going to manufacture it himself. He said he'd already purchased – wait for it – fifty acres of land in Northern Ireland between Dunmurry and Twinbrook, where he's planning to construct an eighty thousand square foot factory!!"

Adams spit on the floor.

Cathel continued. "He's going to call the new car The Delorean DMC 12, and he feels that its innovated gull wing doors, and all aluminium polished body, will make it more popular with the younger generation, than the Mercedes, E-type Jaguar, or the Corvette sports car, and his accountants and production staff compiled statistics, and found that to produce the vehicle would cost exactly two thousand dollars, with the Delorean 12, retailing at twenty five thousand, with full production expected at twenty thousand vehicles a year! "Gentlemen," Cathel visibly excited explained, "work that out – legal money, and the beauty of all this, is that if the IRA finance the factory, we would only employ Catholic workers to fill the three thousand positions needed. Just like the English do in all our factories throughout Northern Ireland with the Protestants. The boot then would be on the other foot, and this would be just the start of it Declan."

Cathel faced the two men in the small room, smoking incessantly, and elaborated once more. "Gentlemen, Kennedy then explained to me that Gallaghers, Northern Ireland's only cigarette manufacturer, that produces a third of the world's cigarettes can you believe – producing seven thousand cigarettes a minute, and with no competition, except from Kennedy's own countrymen. The Americans of course – and he explained that the American Tobacco Company is making a bid to buy out Gallaghers. But he suggested, that if we, the IRA could outbid them, and also become the owners of the Delorean factory, we the IRA would become the biggest employer in Northern Ireland. We could hide the true owners of these companies through Shell corporations, and pay all taxes to mother Ireland instead of the dammed English."

He stared at Adams with pleading eyes. "Can't you see; we will then create a united Ireland without firing a shot."

"Bravo, Bravo!" clapped Adams. "Very interesting. So what would our investment be with this Mr Delorean?"

Cathel smiled. "That's the best part Declan. Sammy Davies Jnr, the American singer, and Johnny Carson, a talk show host in America, have already pledged sixty million dollars towards Delorean's project. That's how good an investment it is."

"Cathel, I'll ask you again!" shouted Adams. "How much would our fucking investment be?"

"ONE HUNDRED AND FIFTY MILLION!" he replied.

Adams vociferously shouted, "Are you out of your fucking mind? Where the fuck do you think we could come up with that kind of money you crazy bastard!"

Cathel smiled again with a contemptuous glare, and said one word. "GADDAFI. Don't you see Declan, nobody will know where the money came from because of the Shell companies we're hiding behind, and Gaddafi would love stickin' it to the English, but I'll tell ya right now Declan, if ya don't go for this deal, Delorean is already talking about approaching the British Government, using the mass unemployment in this country as a leverage to ask them to secure his loan, and I'll tell ya if Westminster give him the money, ya can say goodbye to those three thousand Catholic jobs I talked about."

There was a deathly hush as the room absorbed the silence.

Cathel then started reiterating on the manumit of his people. "Declan, Ireland's biggest export is its people. Six million (Diaspora's) Homogenous Irish live in England and God knows how many live in America. This has got to stop. Let's build our industries and bring them home where they belong, to the land of their birth. For the love of God and Ireland bring them home." Cathel wiped the sweat of his brow with his shirt sleeve and recumbently, seated himself back into the wilted armchair.

Adams obdurately stood with his hands firmly planted on his hips. 'Well, thank you Cathel for your passionate words of wisdom." He then walked over and shook Cathel's hand. "You've certainly given us food for thought and we'll be in touch, you are free to go."

Cathel nodded, and after shaking hands with Collins sauntered out of the farm building, down the muddy concrete steps, and into the cobbled farmyard where his MG stood glistening in the afternoon sunlight, like a celestial escape pod.

"Give him his keys!" shouted Adams to the third Libyan who had not been introduced.

He tossed the keys and Cathel climbed into the sports car and turned on the ignition. He dipped the clutch to engage first gear when General Yahmed poked his leering head, through the open door window.

"I'm sure see you again, Mr Flynn," he smirked, but before he could withdraw his head, Cathel grabbed the General's greasy, black hair, and with his other hand, wound the door glass tightly up on the General's throat, squashing his Adams apple.

He gave the same smirk, at the turbulent General's face that he had received. "Did you know General that smiles are a submissive statement to primates, and they act accordingly."

He sped out of the farmyard with the General's knees flagellating wildly on the gravel road as he was dragged along at speed.

Two hundred yards down the lane, Cathel noticed the Humber giving chase. He slowly turned his head and looked at the General, whose tongue was now grossly extended and turning the same colour purple as the scar on his cheek.

He gave Yahmed a look of complete disgust. "General, the next time you hit someone with a rifle butt, you'd better make sure ya finish the job." He wound down the door glass and elbowed the General in the face, making him perform an undignified exit as he bounced along the grassy shoulder of the lane, where he disappeared into a bramble covered ditch.

"See you later Alligator!" shouted Cathel. "Adios Amigo!"

He accelerated rapidly along the redolently, pleasing lane, inwardly debating to himself about his capricious behaviour.

Chapter 11

Almeria seemed a lifetime away from Northern Ireland, including Cathel's confrontation with the Libyans still floating around in his cranium like a figment of his imagination, an enigma!

He stood and inwardly digested the sun baked terrain that transversed the panoramic windows of his spacious, air conditioned mobile home/dressing room that overlooked the shimmering Spanish landscape.

After two months in the Almeria outback, the extensive location shots were almost complete. The residue of the movie, being filmed on the Universal Studio's sound stage in California. Sergio Leone, the movie's prudent director, had reached the pinnacle of success with his *Fist full of Dollars* spaghetti westerns that he'd elicited and then directed from the original Japanese version entitled *Yojimbo* infuriating its Japanese director, Akira Kurosawa. His 'Dollar' movies usually transformed his actors into megastars like his first spaghetti western had turned an unknown television actor called Clint Eastwood, who previously had played the part of 'Rowdy Yates' in a television cowboy drama named *Rawhide* into an international movie star, but as Cathel pointed out to his friend's, he can't sing though!

Leone's western's made millions, changing the image of 'The Cowboy Movies' forever. Cathel had been cast in his latest epic, as an Irish Gunslinger who rides into town like General Patton about to liberate the French from their German aggressors. His co-stars were a bunch of Italian starlets, and a nondescript American actor called Charles

Bronson, who'd achieved relative fame for his role in an earlier western called *The Magnificent Seven* after spending years in actors' obscurity.

The femme fatale role being portrayed by an English actress named Julie Christie who was cast to play 'Miss Kitty,' the sultry, local saloon keeper.

The gorgeous Christie, with her 'drop dead body' coupled with her intelligence and charm, swooned everyone on the set – mainly in the late afternoons during Cathel's prodigious Vodka' happy hours, and because of Cathel's antics, after hours of inner torment, Leone decided to change the text of the movie from serious to comedic, to everyone's satisfaction, and the stark Almeria landscape soon became bearable and innocuous to all, especially the film crew, with the never ending eye candy of Julie Christie, who's femininity, and sashay around the set, precipitated Leone to contemplate changing the movie's title to *Lust in the Dust*.

General Franco, on being informed of the conglomerate of movie stars that had invaded his presidential shores, invited the recalcitrant ensemble to join him aboard his luxurious (one hundred and ten-ton yacht) *The El Azur* (Goshawk) to celebrate his seventy fifth birthday. They graciously accepted.

The royal Gazelle army helicopter, flew down the rugged coastline of Galicia in northern Spain, like a gargantuan silver Albatross, and after a few seconds hovering, landed on the gleaming teak bow of the majestic yacht.

The star studded entourage alighted the aircraft led by Christie, elegantly draped in some sort of white silk creation, making her appearance being likened to an Egyptian Goddess.

Franco was personally on hand to greet his famous guests, officially attired in all his military regalia, and after shaking hands and bowing, he introduced his party's participants to Julio Englisis – Spain's most popular singer, whose dashing good looks sent Julie Christie's heart all of a flutter as he stood charmingly aloof at the General's side, aboard the gently swaying yacht.

After more lengthy introductions, they were royally escorted and then seated inside a vast dining cabin, where a multitude of gasps reverberated, as everyone absorbed the opulence of the cabin, and the decadence of the table settings. Ten-inch, gold rimmed hunters and solid gold cutlery, glistened extravagantly under cut crystal chandelier droplets, as every delicate course; ENSALADA DE PEPINO (cucumber salad) ESPARRACES BLANCAS EN ACEITE VINAGRE (white asparagus in olive oil and vinegar) SOPA FRIA MENESTRA DE TOMATO – NARANJA VERDURA FRAMBUESA (cold tomato, orange raspberry soup) AL POONDICAS CON SALSA DE PERESIL (meatballs with parsley sauce) COCHINILLO (roast suckling pig) CORDERO ASADO (roast lamb), followed by CRÉME CATALANA, were expertly served.

The ebony, Louie the Fourteenth carved dining tables, with their intricate marquetry tops, and their sturdy twenty-four carat gold corner accents, stood proudly supporting the priceless platters, and gold accessories.

Throughout the gluttonous meal, Cathel kept rudely interrupting by shouting, "Jasus" this food is too good to eat." Which it was – even multimillionaire Leone was unusually impressed, especially with the black bikinied, gold neck-tied waitresses, who were diligently serving the extravaganza. Although he was seething inside, hiding his anger after hearing of the austerity laws handed down to the women of Spain!! They were not allowed a bank account in their own name! They were not allowed mortgages or deeds to a house!! And the one that really frosted him, was the law that stated that if the women's husband should 'die' all assets and monies automatically reverted to their children, sometimes leaving wives and mothers, completely destitute.

The only embarrassing moment of the evening came half way through the meal, when Cathel shouted to the General, "Eh Frank, can ya pass mi the salt!"

But after an awkward silence, and a few giggles, the General smiled and passed him the salt cellar.

On completion of the stupendous dinner, Franco suggested the men retire to the velvet walled lounge (situated to the right of the dining cabin) and join him for an Alvaro cigar and a snifter of Cran Duque d' Alba brandy.

Julio Englisis being the perfect gentleman, offered in his broken English to accompany Julie for a tour of the yacht while the men indulged themselves.

She graciously accepted, with a devilish gleam in her sparkling eyes.

Cathel was calmly relaxing on an ornate Chinese chaise longue, drinking brandy from a pinwheel cut glass snifter, when the General came over and clinked glasses.

"Senor Brendan, I'm so pleased to meet you at last, I've always envied your acting skills, especially the way you project that condescending, arrogant attitude of yours." He smiled. "You remind me so much of me when I was your age."

They both laughed and clinked glasses again.

"I must admit," said Cathel, "this is the best brandy I have ever tasted."

"Of course it is Senor Brendan," replied Franco. "It is after all Spanish and anything Spanish is hard to beat."

Cathel raised his finger. "Except of course the Spanish Armada."

The General gently squeezed Cathel's forearm in

retribution. "Do you know Brendan that my country produces sixty million bottles of brandy a year, and every drop must be aged in oak casks that have been used for at least three years to ferment sherry."

Cathel took another gulp.

"That's why Senor Brendan, whatever type of sherry is aged in the casks, dictates the ultimate colour, taste, and aroma of the brandy. Good yes?"

Cathel put up his hands. "Excuse me, sixty million bottles a year!! Come on General, I think you're exaggerating a little."

He returned a mischievous grin towards Cathel. "How do you think I can afford the petrol for this monstrous boat? Tax Revenue, Brendan, Tax Revenue."

They clinked glasses again.

Franco lit a cigar after offering one to Cathel, which he refused due to the smell of the smoke being reminiscent of his father-in-law. He lit a Park Drive instead.

General Franco put his arm around Cathel's neck. "Now, my new friend Brendan, I have a surprise for you." He pulled down on a gold tassel that hung on the side of the cabin wall. It was strategically attached to a platted silk cord that silently disappeared through a small orifice, in the lounge ceiling.

The louvered, cabin door slid open, and in walked a slender, gaunt faced man, whose features were reminiscent of a person who'd lived a torrid life and only just survived!

He was splendidly dressed in full white navy attire. His short sleeved shirt extenuating his huge tattooed forearms. *Reminiscent,* Cathel thought, *of the cartoon character Popeye.*

The General motioned to Cathel. "I think you know my ship's Captain."

Cathel stood and shook the Captain's hand, a vague

recollection nagging his mind!! Suddenly he recognised him.

"Jasus!! Not Tony McAllister?"

"How you doing Cathel?" said the Captain in a tilted Irish accent.

"Holy shit!" slurred Cathel. "I've not seen ya since we played rugby together at school. How ya doing yourself, and look at you in that pompous outfit, you almost look respectable!"

McAllister twitched with embarrassment, in front of Franco, and slapped Cathel on his shoulder. "What do you say we go for a walk round the poop deck?"

"Jasus Tony," replied Cathel, "that sounds like a line from a Noel Coward play."

McAllister then asked the General's permission to leave, and he waived them aside.

They leaned on the outside chrome railings, ghostly illuminated by the moon's reflection off the rippling surface of the sea.

Mcallister put his hand over Cathel's. "You've certainly done well for yourself since the last time I saw ya, I'll give ya that."

"You'll give me that!" said Cathel in amazement. "What about you!! Captain and First Officer on Franco's yacht? Give me a break." He lightly pinched McAllister's cheek. "The last time I heard of you Tony, was when I read you'd escaped from Maze Prison. Now look at you!"

"It's funny how things turn out, eh Cathel. When my parents forcibly joined me in the Royal Navy for nine years after the RUC caught me making that stupid bomb at sixteen, I had a big grudge against everyone, and everybody. But nine years later, I came out of the navy as a navigation officer, and I must admit, I felt quiet proud of myself, but of course, I made a mistake of going back home didn't I? And once again, got mixed up with the Cause." He stroked his hair in frustration. "I couldn't believe the same shit was still going on, anyway you know the result." He paused. "Shall I just say, I was incarcerated for twenty years, for creating a few minor explosions, but like the Beatles song goes…" He started to sing the first line of the song: "I got out, with a little help from my friends, oh, I got out, with a little help from my friends." He shook his clenched fist in the air in defiance, and proceeded.

"After my escape, the General, who hates England because they won't give Gibraltar back to Spain, heard from his brother-in-law, who is also Irish, can you believe, that I was hiding in Benidorm, and that I had qualifications coming out of my 'Ying Yang' to more than qualify to command his yacht, and BANG, the rest is history."

'Well, I'm pleased for ya Tony mi boy," said Cathel, shaking his hand once again. "And I'm glad, that you're away from all that bullshit, that's happening back home."

McAllister turned and glared at Cathel with a deep searching expression. "To be quite honest Cathel, I'm not really totally away from it all. You see, I'm still a member of the brotherhood, and I'm sort of a steward in their European activity committee – if you know what I mean." He grabbed Cathel's arm. "Cathel, they need people like you and me. People who have easy access to all different countries. You as an actor, and myself as a Captain, who can sail this boat to anywhere I please."

He adopted a smug stance, interlocking his hands behind his back.

"I'm sure you read about the British Embassy being bombed last week in Germany? Guess where the General's yacht was moored?"

"Don't tell me Tony – GERMANY!"

"Exactly!" he retorted, and with a mischievous smile hugged Cathel. "We are going to win independence Cathel, sooner or later because of the efforts of Irishmen like us."

Cathel withdrew a packet of smokes from his shirt pocket and offered McAllister one.

"Don't smoke," he said. "It's bad for your health."

"So's living around people like you," answered Cathel. He proceeded to light his cigarette.

Tony smiled. "Oh by the way Cathel, this will please ya. I've got a diplomatic pouch full of cash for Noraid, compliments of the General, who as you know, religiously loves and embraces Catholicism." He then withdrew, from his rear trouser pocket, a small white envelope (the type you normally find attached to a bunch of flowers) and handed it to Cathel. "I've also got this for ya."

Cathel opened the envelope and perused the parchment gift card inside. His heart started to palpitate as he read...

NO DELOREAN, WE PREFER YOU TO SING...
REGARDS, 'Declan'

He scowled at McAllister, and flipped the card over the chrome railing, and watched as it slowly floated away from the yacht and drifted towards the Gallician coast.

Making a quick move, he grabbed hold of McAllister by his starched shirt and held his angry face, close as he could, to the struggling Captain's face. "Fuck you!" he snarled. "And fuck to your so-called friends!"

He then retreated back down, into the raucous, smoke filled atmosphere, of the lounge.

Chapter 12

The vestry hall of St Anne's Cathedral (in the centre of Belfast) echoed loudly from the grinding sounds of Fender guitars being viciously plucked by the ivory plectrums of Barry Devlin and Charles O'Connor of the Horslips Irish rock band. The motley looking group were belting out a song from their new album entitled, HAPPY TO MEET – SORRY TO PART, which Cathel found so the reverse of his circumstances, after never hearing from Declan Adams since their impromptu meeting at the abandoned farmhouse.

The thought of it transposing itself, every day, into a disgusting, nervous feeling that churned inside his lower bowel tract.

Linda Ronstadt an American singer /music producer /impresario who'd been hired to produce the 'Army Show' cheered and clapped wildly when the Horslips finished their set. "Wonderful, wonderful!" she precipitately screamed.

She turned and faced Cathel who was lounging in an ecclesiastical oak pew behind her.

"Now Brendan if you don't mind, I'd like you to sing your beautiful ballad again but this time..." she shook her hands in front of her as if grasping for something, "...can you put the same passion and feelings into it, like you did when you sang it on *The Old Grey Whistle Test* television show a few months back. You know why Brendan." She leaned over and kissed his left cheek. "Because it was simply amazing. So, let's do it again shall we, and this time try to sing it as though your life depended on it."

Cathel sniggered to himself – if only she knew. Dousing his cigarette in a cold cup of Camp coffee sitting at the end of the pew, he climbed upon the creaking, vestry stage. Manoeuvring his way as he did so, through the vast amount of speakers and amplifiers that were strewn around the stages confined space. Equipment that all three groups of performers – Horslips – Thin Lizzie – and himself, were using for their rehearsals.

He was immediately joined on stage, by a talented young female violinist, who was on loan from the London Philharmonic Orchestra, to play the haunting backing for the ballad he was about to sing, which instantly transformed the otherwise mediocre song into a romantic, chilling experience.

After his performance, he vociferously left the stage still feeling awkwardly tense and emasculated; like he'd felt since arriving back in Northern Ireland, even though everyone in the vestry clapped and whistled loudly at his rendition, including General Sir Harry Tuzo, Commander-in-Chief and Director of Operations for the British Forces, who had been sitting quietly at the rear of the vestry. He was dressed in army fatigues fitted with officer epaulets, observing the whole occurrence. And was now pleasantly surprised as to how the show was proceeding.

The concert had been his idea in the first place to bolster the moral of his troops, after one hundred and thirty British soldiers had been killed in Northern Ireland throughout the year.

The rehearsals wound down to a close, with the General thanking Cathel and offering him a ride in his Vixen Scout Car to the Europa Hotel (on Great Victoria Street) where Cathel had rented the top floor suite for the duration of his stay.

He graciously accepted Sir Harry's offer, reliving in his mind all the road blocks he encountered every day, getting to, and returning from, rehearsals. With most major roads in Belfast cordoned off with Army barricades, in an attempt to thwart car bombings. The camouflaged, painted scout car with its flashing amber roof light, screeched to a halt in a 'No Stopping Zone' outside of the Europa, with Cathel rapidly exiting after thanking the General, and his driver.

He unlocked the door to the hotel suite, and on entering, was greeted by 'Francis' holding a double Jameson's that she gently swished around the rim of a sparkling cut-glass tumbler, as she pouted her exaggerated moist red lips at him.

"Hello Sailor," she said. "Would you like a drink?"

He smiled and roughly placed his arm around her slim waist. They both laughed.

Francis had been seconded in the Europa suite for two days, after receiving the telephone call from Cathel, asking her to join him for a few days during rehearsals, for a show he was about to perform in Belfast. She excitedly accepted his invitation, after telling her manager 'little white lies' about inner women's problems and doctor's appointments, to attain a few days' absence. But after never leaving the suite for two days, she was beginning to feel like 'Anne Frank', although the room service was excellent.

Cathel took a large gulp from the contents of the glass. "So Fran, how was your day?"

She grabbed hold of his hands and smiled into his famous face, kissing him lightly on the lips. "You can see how my day's been," sighed Francis, royally waving with her left arm around the room. "It's the same as you left it?" She playfully pushed him away, a smile starting to erupt at the corners of her voluptuous mouth. "Brendan my love, can we go out tonight for a change? I don't care where, too. The theatre, a restaurant, a bar, anywhere, just get me out of this bloody room!" She ran her fingers though his ruffled hair and sighed. "Brendan, I know you're good at it, but

Christ, you can have too much of a good thing, and to be quite honest, the love making is becoming rather repetitious, apart from making me drier than a parched creek bed, if you know what I mean?"

He smiled, and picking up his drink, gulped once more as she proceeded with her reasoning.

"Brendan, I feel that you're afraid to venture outside with me! Is that it Brendan? I mean, what are you afraid of? Am I that unattractive, that you don't want to be seen with me, or am I here just to be used as a sex object? Or maybe, it's because you don't want to be seen in the company of an older mature women. Is that it Brendan?"

He placed his hands on her shoulders and then slowly stroked her soft taut, feminine neck. "Fran don't talk like that; you know what you're saying is not true. I would surely take you anywhere, but I've a few problems I have to deal with first."

"Really Brendan!" she said, blinking her eyes in doubt! "Well don't you worry yourself, and you have a goodnight, because this problems leaving."

Ten minutes later, the robust hotel door slammed shut with a loud bang, as Francis swaggered down the plush carpeted hall, her striped duffle bag dangling precariously from her right shoulder as she headed for the elevator.

He finished the remnants of his third Jameson's, intently gazing at the framed reproduction of Brandeil's, Rialto Bridge, proudly hanging on the peach coloured wallpaper of the suite.

He faded into his vivid imagination, wishing he was in that romantic gondola, drifting sedately under the ornate bridge, as the tranquil, green waters of the canal, channelled it through the Venetian circle.

What a fool I am, he thought, reprimanding himself for the night's earlier occurrence. He stood and walked over to the window and looked at the wet streets below, shaking his fist at some invisible image. He muttered to himself, "To hell with ya Declan, and ya creepy Generals."

Quickly dressing in a pair of stone washed jeans, and silk black shirt, its pearled buttons twinkling like spotlights beneath the chrome, bathroom track lamps.

He rubbed his setting lotion, soaked fingertips through his ruffled hair in an attempt to tame it a little.

Crossing Greater Victoria Street in front of the Europa, he hurried down the street in search of Francis.

It had rained, and the mercury vapour street lamps cast eerie shadows on the rain-soaked pavements as he entered the Crown Bar at the corner of Greater Victoria and Amelia.

The empty atmosphere of the interior invaded him as he visually scanned the morbid bar.

Two bar flies, seated on high bar stools at the counter, were arguing as to who was paying for the next round, with the bartender scratching his testicle's while reading the local evening paper, totally ignoring the events that were unfolding in front of him.

Cathel abruptly left the establishment.

He turned up the collar on his jean jacket, and on reaching College Square, decided to proceed to Donegal Street and find McGlades.

The streets were deserted, and Cathel couldn't really blame people for not wanting to frequent the bars, after twenty-two bombings had occurred there in the last few months.

McGlades was the in place to go. Where supposedly, all Belfast's youth congregated to dance and sing their blue's away – day or night. And the manager, Paddy Cullen, was known throughout Ireland for his ability to carry five pints of Guinness, unassisted, without a tray!

That's where I'll find Francie, mused Cathel.

The music was blaring out as he approached the bar, after he'd depressingly walked down the dismal Donegal Street. He smiled in anticipation as he opened the front door.

"Sorry fella, we're full," said the overweight, bald headed bouncer who was positioned behind the pub door. His flat broken nose from previous encounters no doubt, menacingly staring at Cathel. The black T-shirt he wore, had LED ZEPPELIN blatantly stretched across his bulging rippled chest, and now he had his large fat hand strategically pressed on Cathel's upper body.

Cathel's face twitched with displeasure. "Listen," he said, pulling a crumpled pound note from his back pocket, "I just want to see if a friend of mine is inside. I'll only take a minute."

The doorman ferociously pushed him backwards, as Cathel attempted to stuff the crumpled money into his hand, to gain entry.

He sat up from his spread eagled position on the wet pavement, as he listened to the bouncer's echoing laughter. He contemplated his next move, and swiftly standing, ran towards the bouncer and grabbing the wire mesh rubbish bin he'd noticed at the side of McGlade's front door, he raised it above his head he brought it down and with all his strength, and rammed it over the shoulders of the surprised doorman, the 'KEEP BRITAIN TIDY' sign fastened to the wire mesh bin, looked so 'apropos' completely obscuring the struggling bouncer's face. Kicking him hard between his legs, Cathel watched as the rubbish bin, with its new occupant, rolled across the pavement and into the wet gutter.

Satisfied, he opened the door once again of the crowded bar, and was about to enter when the RUC officer's truncheon viciously struck him on the back of his head, with a sickening thud!

119

Chapter 13

The smell of urine was overwhelming as he lay, facedown, on the cold, vibrating metal floor of the police van. His hands firmly handcuffed behind his back, as the vehicle sped towards the #19. RUC station on Rosemary Street, in the middle of Belfast town centre. The flood of concentrated fresh air, permutated his senses, when the rear doors of the 'Black Maria' suddenly creaked open and Cathel found himself being roughly dragged out of his smelly cage.

He was supported, underneath his clammy armpits by strong, muscular, gloved hands, and frog marched across the dark, dismal, cobbled stoned courtyard of the police station, and into the harshly illuminated, yellowing light of the station's interior that intentionally concealed, the ancient looking charge office counter, its shoddy wooden top, showing scratches and gouge's from neglect and abuse.

"Stand up straight in front of the sergeant, you slovenly bastard!" shouted one of the arresting officers, as he kicked Cathel hard on his right shin.

Cathel slowly raised his head off his blood stained, jean jacket collar, and stared directly at the burly charge office sergeant, who was seated behind the enormous monstrosity of a desk.

He stared back at Cathel with a surprised look on his face, his bloated red cheeks reminded Cathel of a South American Blow fish; pleasant to look at, but deadly poisonous inside?

"So what do we have here?" said the sergeant, still

intensely staring at Cathel.

"Arrested for causing a mischief Sergeant," said one of the officers.

"Had to subdue him because of his violence," said the other.

The sergeant slammed the pen he was holding, loudly on the desk top, while giving the two arresting officers a nonchalant smile. "Shall I rephrase myself gentlemen?" he replied. "I should have said – who do we have here?"

Both police officers gazed across at each other and then back at the sergeant completely mystified by his comments.

"Gentlemen," the sergeant proceeded, "did you search the prisoner for ID or weapons at the point of arrest, as per usual?" He glared at both officers.

"No sergeant," said the tall one. "We wanted to get him off the street before he caused any more trouble?"

"Is that right?" answered the sergeant, as he noticed Cathel smiling at him. He stood from behind his desk, his six foot four, and two hundred and fifty pounds' stature, overshadowing the three men in front of him. He leaned forward and directed his remarks to the police officers, "Gentlemen. Have either of you been laid off without pay, for wrongful arrest charges being brought against you?"

They both stared defiantly at the 'Blow fish'.

"We've no idea what the hell ya talking about Sergeant," they both said in unison.

"Really?" he said. "Well, have either of you two 'pouting' officers ever seen the movie *The Sport of Giants* or the motive *Horse*?"

"Of course we have!" said the taller of the two again. "But I'll wager, so has all of bloody Ireland I should imagine. So what's that got to do with anything Sergeant?"

Both officers stood there stultified.

"Well. Mr intelligent police officers, just take a wee minute and have a look at your prisoner's face, and then answer your own question? But… before you do, I suggest you un-cuff him, because when his solicitor gets here, I think you'll be charged with using excessive force and unnecessary assault during the course of an arrest?"

The police officer who'd clubbed Cathel with his black oak truncheon, turned and visually absorbed Cathel's smiling face, and omitted a loud gasp. "Jasus Christ! Mother of God! It's Brendan Flynn!" He hurriedly un-cuffed Cathel between a plethora of excuses escaping from his mumbling mouth. "I'm so sorry Mr Flynn," he said. "But ya can sees how easy it was to make a mistake, what with the darkness and drizzle and all. And seeing the bouncer rolling down Donnagal Street in that wire basket?" He smiled. "Which ya don't see every day by the way? And we knew that if his friends had come out of McGlades and seen what you'd done to him, we would have had a riot on our hands, if ya know what I mean?"

The sergeant just sat there with his arms folded, absorbing every minute of the conversation. A quiet moment then ensued.

"Now Mr Flynn," said the sergeant, "I must apologise for my men, but you can see it was a genuine mistake." He came from behind his desk, and stood behind Cathel to examine the back of his head. "Firstly Mr Flynn, we should take you to the infirmary, just in case you need stitches in this wound of yours?"

Cathel turned, and, grabbing hold of the sergeant's hand, said, "Firstly if ya don't mind I'd like a cigarette?" He then struggled to remove from his back trouser pocket a crushed, sodden, red and white packet of Park Drives, and pulled a face at the dilapidated, wet contents? "I don't suppose that any of yus have a Park Drive I can have do you? 'Cause it looks like that fat bastard bouncer annihilated these."

A scrambling sea of blue uniforms scattered, like a flock of disturbed pigeons, and within seconds, a policeman swaggered over to Cathel and presented him with a Park Drive cigarette, and after Cathel placed it between his lips, produced a box of Swan Vesta matches, and proudly lit it for him.

Cathel inhaled deeply and slowly exhaled the smoke as though it was the most exciting thing he'd done in years? He turned towards the big man in charge and said, "I'm sorry Sarg, but I'm going to have to decline your offer of the infirmary, but, I wouldn't mind a ride to the Europa Hotel."

The sergeant grabbed hold of Cathel's hand once more, and shaking it vigorously said, "No problem Mr Flynn? I'll have a car waiting out front in a few minutes, and 'Sir', if anyone asks ya for your autograph, I'll personally, fuckin kill em."

Cathel smiled.

The next day, he headed back to Portadown, nursing a massive headache as he lounged in the back seat of the hire car, his driver nonchalantly coasting the vehicle along the uneven roads.

After being dropped off at the Europa the night before by a police vehicle, he'd proceeded directly to his suite expecting to find Francis, but to no avail.

The hotel doctor attended to his wound while he telephoned Linda Ronstadt to explain the predicament he now found himself in.

She completely understood, and said she would cancel the rest of the week's rehearsals and reschedule for the following week, and after wishing him well, hung up the phone.

At that, he lay on the huge queen-size bed in his room,

and fell into a fast, agitated sleep.

His plan had been to stop at the Automotive Associations office on the High Street in Portadown, on the way home to his cottage, and apologise to Francis. But on his arrival, caused quite a 'stir' when he entered their offices.

He was informed that she'd called in sick a few days earlier, and was taking the rest of the week off. So after kissing the hands of all the female staff, which was now expected of him due to the publicity he had always received for such an innocuous idiosyncrasy, he signed a few autographs and proceeded on his way.

He inserted his key into the front door lock of the cottage on his arrival, and was surprised to find it open!!

"Not again!" he said to himself.

He sauntered in and looked around expecting to find Pedigrew, or some other conspicuous person, but the cottage was empty.

And then he saw it!

Sitting on the dining room table was a brown cardboard box, with a popular sauce manufactures logo on all four sides. The flaps on the top were untidily fastened down with beige masking tape.

He slowly circled the table a few times, while not taking his eyes of the foot square carton and debated to himself whether to open it or not?

He released a subliminal sigh and spontaneously ripped off the masking tape, and to his surprise, nothing exploded, except his heart rate!! He pulled open the top flaps that inwardly revealed a large clear plastic bag.

He stopped, and looking at the bag, lit another cigarette and pondered his next move. Eventually, he took the cigarette from his mouth and placed it into a side ashtray, and then slowly opened the plastic wrapping.

Inside, he found a large white Tupperware bowl, its lid tightly sealed. He gently extracted the bowl and placed it on the wobbly, dining table, as his heart pounded rapidly inside his chest. He then forced open the lid, aided with pressure from his thumbs under the outer lip. It released a slight gushing sound, and omitted a pungent, food odour as the seal was broken.

He looked at the large piece of succulent red meat inside the bowl; at first glance looking like an expensive round of Tenderloin.

"Why would anyone send me a piece of meat?" he said to himself.

He inserted both hands underneath the Tenderloin and lifted it clear of the bowl, turning it over as he did so.

He would never remember what he saw first? Was it the mauve, protruding nipple, or the swallow tattoo?

All he remembered, was dropping the eviscerated breast back into the white Tupperware bowl, and screaming in an octave he'd never used before.

He rushed into his small compact kitchen, and stopping at the white vitreous enamel sink, turned both faucets fully open, and ferociously immersed his tainted hands into the gushing water as falling tears blurred his vision.

Two double Jameson's, and four chain smoked Park Drives later, he regained his composure and returned to the gruesome Tupperware, and sadly gazed down at the dissected contents.

He gingerly raised the white bowl with extended arms, and attempted to replace it back inside its cardboard tomb, when suddenly he noticed another plastic bag concealed beneath the plastic wrapping.

He delicately placed the bowl on the dining table, and

reaching inside the box, removed the second plastic bag, which turned out to be, two, three-inch-wide strips of clear Sellotape, and the tape appeared to be at least a foot long, and strategically folded in half.

He put his hand over his mouth and gasped in horror, as he unfolded the Sellotape strips? There, grotesquely suspended between the firmly sealed strips, were the outer labia of a female's genitalia, badly bruised and inflamed, and at the top section of the strip, encapsulated between the glued layers, lay a large clump of meticulously arranged, ginger pubic hairs!

Emotion overcame him again, as he nervously rubbed his fingers through his tussled hair and down the sides of his inwardly drawn, tear stained cheeks as he morosely pondered the immolation of Francis.

He eyes then caught the sight of a piece of white, folded paper, lying at the bottom of the box. The name 'CATHEL' glaring up at him from the outside fold of the white vermillion.

Cathel sank to his knees when his shaking, nervous fingers removed the note, and he reluctantly read what was written inside the fold. It said:

ENJOY... I KNOW WE DID...

Chapter 14

English Cocker Spaniel Wanted
Must have Kennel Club Certification Reply Box no 348

Major Pedigrew Jennings drove down Union Street, in a nondescript, old Ford Consol as he headed towards Shankill graveyard. Dressed as usual in the shabby clothes he always wore when entering 'Enemy Territory'.

After scouring the want ads in the *Belfast Times* the previous morning; as he did most days – there it was – the coded message that he'd informed Cathel to insert in the newspaper, if ever he needed assistance!

It had been two days since Cathel had morosely spent, recovering from the initial abhorrence of receiving Francis's dissected body parts, and after consuming more alcohol on that dreadful day, had contacted Adams by telephone and screamed threatening obscenities down the mouthpiece at him, blaming the evisceration of Francis on General Ali Yahmed. But after his rantings had subsided, somewhat! Adams had politely apologised, and sympathetically explained that he had no control over General Yahmed whatsoever, and that the General was allowed to carry out his assignments in Ireland as he saw fit, and advised Cathel to keep well away from him, as he was a ruthless individual who hated Cathel's guts, and Francis was a warning to him to cooperate with the Brotherhood, or else!

Cathel suddenly cut Adams off in midsentence with a

stream of vicious vulgarities before slamming down the phones receiver, and, after inwardly dissecting his tumultuous predicament, instinctively telephoned the wanted ad number of the *Belfast Times*.

Pedigrew methodically inspected the severed body parts, before replacing them in to the small fridge in Cathel's kitchen. He scratched the end of his chin in disbelief. Turning, he addressed Cathel. "I'm sorry for your loss Brendan old boy and I'll certainly dispose of those items for you, but tell me, what do the Brotherhood expect you to do for them, that they would go to such extreme measures, as too dissect your friend!"

Cathel gave Pedigrew a soulful look. "I have a vague idea what they expected from me, but I'll let you know when I'm positive."

The Major smiled and intensely gazed at Cathel, trying to read his reactions. "You wouldn't be holding something back from me would you Brendan?" He took a deep breath. "You've seen what they're capable of, and I would hate for something nasty to befall you my friend. We know about the Libyans, and we also know that you were detained by them some time ago, and I promise you Brendan, if they are threatening you in some way, we have ways of dealing with them, but you must come clean with us, there's a good chap."

Cathel removed a Park Drive from the wooden cigarette box sitting on top of his coffee table, and striking a match down the side of his jeans, lit the slow burning tobacco.

"I thought you didn't smoke in your cottage?" exclaimed Pedigrew.

Cathel expelled a cloud of smoke from his mouth. "I never used to Mr bloody Pedigrew Jennings, until you turned my perfect life upside down. Now look at me! I'm a shadow of my former, famous self."

Pedigree put his arms around Cathel as he watched tears begin to shroud his piecing blue eyes. He gave him a comforting hug.

A few seconds passed before Cathel broke away and smiled at Pedigrew. "I'll tell you this Major, if a hidden paparazzi had just taken a photo of us just then, we'd both be in big shit!"

They both laughed haughtily.

Cathel rubbed the moisture from the corner of his eyelids and decided to have a change of heart, and started to explain his meeting with Adams and the Generals. Making no mention of the concert, but outlined the plan he'd proposed about Delorean and Gallaghers.

Still full of doubt, Pedigrew asked, "Why would they kill your girlfriend over a business deal?"

Cathel chewed at the inside of his lower lip in frustration, before answering. "I think they had other plans in the works, but when I brought up the Delorean deal, it gave them food for thought, but I think they killed Fran to let me know that they are still in charge."

Pedigrew stroked his chin once again, in deep thought. "Okay," he said. "I think these devious gentlemen have something planned for you, and I think you have an inclination of what it is. And I know you feel inside that if you inform on your IRA friends, you'll feel like a traitor to Northern Ireland. But will you?" He placed his hands in his shabby jacket pockets and paced the room while continuing talking. "Brendan… it's no longer your Irish friends we're talking about! We are talking about Libyan thugs who have no right being in your precious country, so if you have something to tell me, please tell me now, so's we can neutralise these thugs once and for all. Please Brendan, for the love of Ireland."

Cathel couldn't believe Pedigrew's dilettante attitude and suddenly grabbed hold of him, his thumb and forefinger grasping tightly on the Major's throat. Pedigrew didn't resist, he just stood there motionless, staring at the inside wall of the cottage as though in a trance!

"Listen you Pommie bastard! Don't try to push that Irish fuckin guilt trip on me. You don't give a shit what happens to Northern Ireland, or my Catholic friends." He could feel his fingers tightening around Pedigrew's neck. "It's just a job to you, and I'm sure all you're thinking about, is the accolades you'll receive from your bosses in London if you can somehow avert this looming disaster, so go fuck yourself Pedigrew and let me fight my own battles."

"Disaster!" screamed Pedigrew. "What fucking disaster are you referring to, Brendan?" He folded his arms in front of him and waited for an answer, as he closely examined Cathel's sneering face.

The Mexican standoff lasted but seconds, with both men's eyes locked firmly on each other.

Pedigrew then swiftly pulled the offending hand off his neck and turning, headed for the cottage door. On reaching the door he stopped and looked at Cathel. "Don't forget who contacted who Brendan? Put the remains of Francis in the outside rubbish bin, and one of my men disguised as a dustman, will retrieve them sometime in the next few days." He fastened his dilapidated overcoat as he vacated the cottage and shouting over his shoulder said, "Good luck Brendan, you'll need it!"

After depositing the bodily remnants in the outside, rubbish receptacle, Cathel made up his mind not to be intimidated with Adams or the Generals ever again and decided to seek out the Generals before they did the same to him?

Surprise is of the essence, he told himself. A line he had fastidiously rehearsed when he'd used it in one of his movies, and it had sounded so good when he had spoken the words so reverently in front of the camera. 'Surprise is of the essence'.

The sun became a misty blur behind the drifting clouds as the MG Midget came to an abrupt stop at the side of Randle's farm. He heaved himself out of the low slung sports car and gazed around at the magnificent landscape. The Mountains of Mourn were standing menacingly erect in the distance, their purple green patina shrouded in a moisturised blanket of Cumulus. He thought back to the last time he was there, when he'd been apprehended by the Humber. He then tried to remember how long the impromptu journey had taken, while being hooded and forcibly driven, in the back seat of the 'Super Snipe'.

He estimated his conversation with Adams had taken approximately thirty minutes when he'd looked down at his wrist watch after dumping the General so undignified, into the drainage ditch. The black fingers, on the white faced watch registered 11.55. Deducting the thirty-minute meeting off the travel time, and remembering being corralled in his car by the cows at eleven, he deduced that if he drove down the lane for twenty-five minutes he would be in the vicinity of the farmhouse. He knew that if he'd driven towards it from the bottom of the dale, the way that he'd left so hurriedly on that day, he could have easily been seen for miles, as the farmhouse had strategically been built on a rocky mound at the top of the hill, giving it a panoramic view of the whole resplendent valley. *Hence the reason*, thought Cathel, *that the property was purchased in the first place.*

He started his car, and sliding it in gear, slowly drove down the lane for twenty minutes, then suddenly he turned the steering wheel and accelerated towards a small grassy knoll at the side of dense shrubbery and low hanging trees.

He switched off the ignition when his vehicle was completely hidden beneath the greenery, and after making up his mind, walked the last half mile or so, just in case the noise of the car aroused suspicion.

He clambered over a dilapidated stile, that gave access over the top of a rustic fence, that surrounded the periphery of the farmyard, and diving into long grass growing between the fence and a row of tall trees, he removed a pair of binoculars from the inside pocket of his leather jacket and scanned the surroundings.

The first thing that came into his optical assisted vision was the maroon Humber, it's long obtrusive front, blatantly jutting out from behind an elongated cowshed. He waited for visible signs of human activity – nothing.

Creeping through the grass he edged his way to the corner of the nearest building, his heart beating wildly. Gauging the distance from himself to the farmhouse to be less than forty feet, he swiftly ran towards it, and reaching the rear of the building, flattened his body tightly against the pebble dash coating of the exterior.

Breathing heavily, he gingerly turned the handle on the rear door and pulled at it, surprisingly it was unlocked!

He silently climbed the obnoxious smelling staircase in front of him, withdrawing as he did so; from his side jacket pocket, the Mesula, chrome pistol that Pedigrew had accidentally left behind on his coffee table after his first unannounced visit to his cottage.

He wrapped his sweaty fingers around the Stag horn handle of the pistol grip and proceeded up the staircase to the room above.

He pressed his ear against the flush plywood door at the top of the stairs, and hearing high rate voices deep in conversation that drifted through the cracks in the warped plywood, decided to make his move!

Grabbing the well-worn door knob with his right hand, while tightly gripping the chrome pistol with his left, he burst into the room. Antiquated 'Shillelagh' hit his hand with exerted force, making the pistol noisily slide across the uneven planked floor.

He never had a chance to see his assailant hiding behind the door, before the large fist; wrapped in a black leather glove, connected with the left side of his face, making him collapse in a defeated heap in the centre of the room, with the five men who stood around him, clapping loudly as Cathel attempted to stand.

"Good morning Cathel," said Declan Adams, menacingly standing over him. "Decided to drop in for lunch did you?"

The room echoed with laughter as General Ali Yahmed removed the glove from his throbbing hand and replaced it with a Russian, Makarov pistol, which he pointed at Cathel, and waited for Adams to speak.

"How stupid do you think we are Cathel?" said Adams. "We all knew you'd turn up here eventually, and the tracking device that one of the General's planted in your little car the last time you were here, sure helped us to know when."

"Look," said Rory Collins, pointing to a small grey metal box perched on an empty orange crate at the far end of the room. "See that flashing yellow light on the screen Cathel, that's your car. And see those numbers illuminated on the bottom of the screen, that's how far away your vehicle is from this building." He stepped closer to Cathel, who was gently rubbing the side of his cheek. "Clever eh, Cathel?" He smiled. "Mind you, we thought we'd lost you when you stopped a mile or so up the lane, until that is, the remote motion detector fastened to the roof of one of the outbuildings, picked up a movement at the outer perimeter fence. And there you were, on that other screen, doing that magnificent dive off the top of the stile into the grass." He laughed again. "We all cheered at that Cathel."

His eyes showed distain as he listened to Collins.

General Yahmed in his licentious swagger, came towards Cathel, and standing in front of him, lowered his pistol to his side. "Sorry about woman," he said, "she's just casualty of war."

Cathel's famous head-butt slammed into the bridge of Yahmed's nose, exploding a deep two-inch gash that bloodily pumped open, a ragged split down the full length of his aquiline features.

"Ah... you son of bitch!" screamed the General. He raised the pistol to Cathel's head, while trying to stem the flow of blood from his nose using his shirt sleeve.

Cathel smiled. "Oh... I'm sorry General, did that hurt?"

The furious General cocked the trigger on his Makarov pistol and pressed it into Cathel's left ear.

Adam's silently raised and pointed, a Colt '357' Magnum revolver at Yahmed and politely said, "Ali, if he goes, you go with him?"

Yahmed looked at Adam's with venom seeping from his wide, mahogany brown eyes, and then smirking back at Cathel, disengaged the trigger, which released a deadly 'click' that resonated around the shocked room.

"My turn it will be next Mr Flynn. My turn next!" he snarled, as he continued to try and stem the flow of blood with his thumb and index finger as it dripped on the wooden floor.

Adam's replaced his outrageously large barrelled revolver, into its brown leather shoulder holster strapped to his upper torso, and beckoned Cathel to be seated.

Yahmed walked out of the room in disgust, followed by his two subordinate officers.

"Well that was certainly interesting," said Adam's, a mischievous smile slowly breaking across his face. "And I'm sure the General is pissed off with me now, as much as he is with you, but we've come too far with this operation to now lose our main participant!" He saluted Cathel. "Anyway, listen to what I have to say, because this is an outline of the plan which is proceeding nicely."

He unfolded a large blueprint and laid it on the table top in front of Cathel and Collins and cleared his throat.

"Now gentlemen, this is a blueprint that we have illegally acquired, of the hangar at the Thiepval barracks where the concert is taking place." Using his finger as a pointer, he explained certain aspects of it. "These white crosses that you see gentlemen, are the twenty support pillars that the outer shell of the hangar was constructed upon. They are the only structural supports for the entire building."

Cathel lit a cigarette, trying not to show his waning interest in the conversation.

Adam's proceeded. "As I said, the plan has already been activated, and this will really surprise you Cathel. We found out that Linda Ronstadt, the producer of the show, was telephoning around town, looking for a reputable bonded haulage contractor to remove all the equipment from the vestry hall at St Ann's Cathedral, that was to be used for the concert, and wanted it to be subsequently taken to the Thiepval barracks in Lisburn.

"So we asked a certain friend of mine, who runs Anderson Haulage – the largest haulage contractor in Belfast, to telephone Ronstadt and explain that he'd heard (down the grapevine) that she was looking to hire a haulage contractor, and to offer her a price she couldn't refuse!! Needless to say, she greedily accepted."

Cathel could see by Adam's agitated movements that he was getting visually excited.

"Yesterday," he murmured, "some of our members, who also work for Andersons, arrived at the vestry hall in two sign painted cube vans that said ANDERSONS in bright yellow, cleverly depicted in blue outline that made the name brilliantly stand out on both sides of the vehicles. They then proceeded, under Ronstadt's direction, to load eight huge speaker cabinets, four amplifiers, a multitude of extension cables, spools of speaker wires, and two futuristic looking sound boards with metal stands, into the back of the vans. "But wait!" he excitedly said. "The best is yet to come... she gave the foreman of the crew Patrick Jenkins, a government army pass to enable the vans to enter the barracks unmolested, and guess what Cathel? It was signed by the Commander-in-Chief, General, Sir Harry Tuzo."

Cathel waited for Adam's to shout 'Whoopee' or some other superlative adjective like his body language said he was about too, but instead, became exceedingly agitated and carried on with his irritable speech.

"So, the men were busy loading the vans while Jenkins who fancies himself as a lady's man, was chatting to Ronstadt, and he accidentally on purpose, mentioned that if she hadn't already found someone to mount the speakers in the correct locations to acoustically balance them, he knew of a sound technician who lived in Belfast. A member of Rod Stewart and the Faces entourage, who installs all the sound equipment for Rod at every one of the Faces tour concerts, and he makes sure the control consoles, the microphones, and the speakers are all in sync. Ronstadt couldn't believe her luck, and telephoned him there and then, and of course, Cathel, he's Catholic and a sympathiser to our cause." Adams pumped his fist in the air.

"What's the acoustics, and this Rod Stewart thing got to do with anything?" asked Cathel.

Adams smiled again and leaning over, placed his hand on Cathel's arm. "Cathel, the beauty of all this, is that Ronstadt gave instructions that the equipment be delivered to the barracks the following day. So yesterday afternoon, the vans after leaving the vestry, drove directly to a warehouse we own, and throughout the afternoon and night, the speaker cabinets were dismantled by Yahmed and his team, and two pound slabs of Semtex along with electrolytic capacitors and boosters were installed into each cabinet, and then the two, twelve inch speakers were repositioned into their original brackets and the backings were secured with breakoff bolts, so's that if anybody tried to tamper with the cabinets, by removing the bolts, the bolt heads break off on the first turn, leaving the speakers tamper proof." He took a deep, satisfactory breath. "The amazing thing about Semtex plastic explosive's Cathel, is that it can't be detected by sniffer dogs or x-rays, so you can see it suits all our needs. Then, on completion of the speakers, our Rod Stewart man plugged them in to make sure there was no distortion, and guess what?" He eagerly grabbed hold of Cathel's other arm. "They worked perfectly!"

Cathel broke from his grasp and stood away from the table, and the offending blueprint. "Declan, if you think I'm going to stand anywhere near those speakers you've got another thing coming, because I'm sure, that after two to three hours of rehearsals, the transformers in the speaker boxes must get pretty hot, and who knows how that will affect a slab of bloody Semtex?"

"Cathel, Cathel, Cathel!" screamed Adam's. "It's a damn good job you make money as an actor, because I'm thinking you'd be useless at anything else? Don't you realise, that's why we have the capacitors to detonate the Semtex. You can shoot at that shit and it won't explode, so don't worry about a stupid transformer. So calm yourself will ya."

Cathel sat back down and lit another Park Drive, not knowing how to become detached from this odious situation he found himself in.

Adam's came back to the table and spreading the blueprint out once more pointed to three white x's, marked on either side of the drawing. "These x's are where the speakers are going to be mounted on the support pillars, and two will be placed on the stage with the amplifiers. Are you following this, Cathel?"

He nodded his head in disgust.

"The configuration of the speakers has been mathematically worked out by an explosive expert - Yahmed! So's that the sympathetic detonation when activated will implode the whole building."

"Okay, that's enough!" shouted Cathel, jumping away from the table. "I've told ya, I don't want anything to do with this shit, and I'm surprised you do too, Declan? You've done amazing things for the Provo's since we split from the 'Mother load' in '69'. But this Declan! This is mass murder!"

Adam's thumped his fist loudly on top of the blueprint. "Cathel, this is fucking warfare! Don't you think that if the English could find a way to annihilate four thousand Provo's, in one fell swoop, they'd do it!! "You bet they would. They've been doing it for years. In India, South Africa, Malaysia, Cyprus, and any other county that they supposedly colonised. And listen, don't ever let me regret stopping the General from shooting you, because, to be quite honest, I don't like his methods, but he certainly gets things done, and what we are about to do, will go down in history for the sheer magnitude of deaths achieved by a second rate army against a superior force, and I'm sorry Cathel, but your name will never be implicated with our glory and nobody will ever know that without you, we could never have succeeded."

"Really... well that's very nice of you Declan. Is that because I'll be 'dead', most probably killed by the first explosion?"

Adam's inhaled. "Listen Cathel. You'll be nowhere near the hangar at the time of the implosion. The show will commence at eight pm. And at seven fifty, the control panel switch will be activated, sending a signal to the timers

139

hidden in the amplifiers, which in turn will send a power surge to the capacitors in two second intervals, which in turn will detonate sixteen pounds of Semtex. Our Rod Stewart man will vacate the hangar once he's activated the switch, on pretence of fetching more equipment. But I'm afraid Ronstadt, who will be onstage introducing the first act, and also the Horslips, who will be the first act, will have to be sacrificed. But you Cathel, being the last performer on the program, will say your transport broke down on the way to the show and that's why you were nowhere near the hangar when the catastrophe happened."

Cathel felt physically and mentally sick. He stood and slouched over to the open door he'd entered from at the top of the stairs. "I'm leaving now before I do something stupid again Declan, so I'll talk to you later."

Adam's intently stared at Cathel and shook his head. "Just remember Cathel what happened to your woman, and I also think you may start running out of friends if you don't do as you're told? I can't protect you forever, unless of course, we can rely on you and your silence. We need you, and your Country needs you!"

"Fuck you Declan!" he shouted, and after retrieving his Mesula pistol, headed down the smelly staircase to attain his exit from the farmhouse.

Chapter 15

'MAY START RUNNING OUT OF FRIENDS', Cathel mulled the statement over in his mind as he entered the outskirts of Lurgan in his sports car.

On walking back to his hidden vehicle from the tense situation in the farmhouse, he'd opened the car doors and lifted out the rear dickey seat and searched underneath. Nothing. He then searched underneath the front seats, even in between the webbing supports and hog rings. Nothing. He removed the spare wheel from the 'boot' and searched the surrounding areas, also running his hands underneath the rear parcel shelf and around the inner locking support panel. Nothing.

Moving to the outside surface of the vehicle, he scoured the inners of the front wings. Nothing. Until, he eventually made his way to the rear of his car, and there it was, magnetically adhered to the left rear quarter, inner wheel arch. Concealed with dust, and highway grime – a small, black, bakelite box with a minute flashing red light mounted on the right front corner still in motion!!

He grimaced and stared at it in his hand before slamming it hard on the ground. Then, lifting his foot, stomped on the offending unit, crushing it into a million pieces.

Looking down at the shattered bakelite mingled with the thin wires and transistors, reminded him of the remote controlled car he'd purchased for his son one Christmas, and five minutes after Patrick had unwrapped the gift, he'd pulled back on the remote joystick and watched in horror as the plastic racing car careened at speed, off the back deck of the Priory, with everyone present running towards the edge of the upper deck, to sadly gaze down at the scattered remnants of the toy and its inner workings.

Cathel felt that same awful Deja vu feeling again, as he looked down at the demolished tracking unit at his feet.

What did Adam's mean – 'start running out of friends'?

Suddenly he slammed on the brakes, making the little car zigzag on the slippery road as the thought came to him? 'RORY MURPHY'.

He frantically headed towards Portadown and the McConville, making the six-mile trip in ten minutes.

Screeching to a halt in the flag-stoned car park, he jumped out of the MG and ran to the front door of the pub that was still dominated by its ridiculously large wrought iron, black medieval hinges, and finding it locked, looked at his wrist watch and realised it was afternoon closing time.

Making his way to the rear of the building, he let himself inside the gloomy premises through a rear side door used for deliveries, and after desperately searching all the street level rooms for Rory, including the snug and tap room, descended down the stone steps into the damp cellar, hitting his head on the way down, on a bare bulb hanging hauntingly from the plaster ceiling, making it sway violently on its foot long wired socket, transposing his illuminated, larger than life shadowed silhouette, onto the whitewashed pealing walls.

And there he was, tapping the beer lines that straddled the huge hooped barrels lying on their sides in the damp atmosphere. He was busily cleaning out the stagnant beer residue that sometimes clogged the plastic lines which made the upstairs pumps squirt haphazardly, instead of the normal expected flow.

He smiled on seeing Cathel, and walking over, gave him the usual 'Bear Hug.'

Cathel reciprocated, and then did something he'd never done to Rory before! He grabbed hold of both sides of his head and kissed him fully on the mouth!

"What the fuck was that all about?" he yelled, spitting on the flagstone floor, as though in disgust.

"Rory, I'm just so pleased to see you."

"Well thank you Cathel, but it's not like we haven't seen each other in a while. I'd dread to think what you'd be planning to do to me if you ever went away for a year or so?" He laughed.

They went upstairs to the empty snug, with friendly arms clasped around each other. Rory attempted to pull two pints of Guinness from the brass pumps but nothing came out except gurgling froth, because as he explained to Cathel, he'd disturbed the plastic pump lines while cleaning. Eventually they both cheered when the third pint came out perfect, with the black liquid nicely settling down beneath its usual inch high head of foam.

They sat and slurped at their Guinness, with Cathel intermittently sipping at a Piper Export out of the bottle.

They discussed the latest bombings and atrocities that had been happening locally and during their conversation, Rory mentioned he'd had an interesting occurrence happen in the bar.

"It's funny that you should call in so soon after this incident Cathel, but the other day, two swarthy looking men with foreign accents came in, and all they ordered was lemonade and orange juice, but as they leaned against the bar, one of the men who had a large purple scar down his left cheek, asked me in broken English if this was the bar that you frequented, and when I answered, 'occasionally', he then said, 'I hope you insured'. Then they drank up and left. Don't you find that weird Cathel?"

He asked Rory to pull him another pint, lugubriously deciding whether to admit he knew the men in question or shrug it off. "Rory... I need to talk to you about something," he said, when he placed the fresh pint in front of him.

"After kissing me, I suppose now you're going to tell me you love me? Honestly Cathel, you bloody actors are all alike."

"No please," he said. "Sit down for a minute and be serious, I've something to tell ya." He thought for a moment on how much information to divulge. "Rory, the two men you've just talked about... I know them." He fidgeted on his stool. "They're from Libya and are here helping the Brotherhood, and they are nasty people Rory, so don't mess with them."

He paused and lit a cigarette before proceeding.

"They're asking me to do something for them that I'm dead set against doing, and I think they came in here to let me know, that no one who I care about is safe until this thing is over, and to do what I'm told."

Rory rubbed at his forehead while staring across at Cathel. "Why don't you just tell them to go fuck themselves or you're going to inform the Garda about them. Not the RUC of course, they're all protestants?"

"Are you joking?" replied Cathel. "I'll wager most police, no matter who, are in their pockets!! "You don't understand Rory, they don't worry about killing people, they don't differentiate between men, women, children, it's all the same to them. That's why I'm not going to tell you anymore, or it may put your life in jeopardy." He leaned over and whispered, "I'm explaining this to you, so's that you're aware of these gutless bastards, and to stay well away from them. Do you understand?" He placed his hand over Rory's that held the pint pot. "Rory, I've lost Kieran because of the shit that's happening here and I don't want to lose you the same way? So don't start anything if you see them again. I know you and your temper, and I'm

144

telling you, they fight dirty, so please don't dare start anything, because you can't beat them, and trust me, I'll sort this shit out my own way?"

"But there must be something I can do to help Cathel?"

He gently slapped Rory on the cheek. "You can help me by staying alive, and when this is all over I'm going to buy you a nice fancy bar. Nothing like this rat hole Rory, I'm talking a nice bar."

Rory jokingly pushed him off the bar stool. "To hell with you Cathel, this pub can never be replaced! Feel it Cathel, feel it, the ambience. It's all around us like a warm cuddly blanket, money can't replace that feeling... it's called nostalgia."

Cathel smiled and kissed Rory once again. "See you my friend, love ya."

"Likewise," said Rory, as they parted company.

Chapter 16

The red capped, army guard asked Cathel to please wait on the outside perimeter of the barbed wired entrance to the barracks, and with an abrupt about turn, marched away, while the secondary, red capped military policeman, stood sternly at attention, his sub machine gun at the ready.

Cathel knew the soldier was watching him, but couldn't be certain, as the neb on the soldier's cap was strategically covering his eyes!!

Cathel sat there, in his car, and after lighting a cigarette, slid an eight track into its player and slowly released a mouth full of smoke as he listened to the soothing voice of Dean Martin drifting up from the track player mounted underneath the dashboard, as he waited to gain entry to the heavily guarded compound of the Thiepval Barracks.

Fifteen minutes later, the Redcap returned to the window of the MG and clicking his heels on the asphalt drive, saluted Cathel and presented him with a yellow, hand written card.

"Next time sir," he said, "would you apply for a pass before you get here, if you don't mind. It saves a lot of time and inconvenience." He lowered his head closer to the cars open door glass. "I recognised your face, Sir, but orders are orders."

Cathel slid two fingers around the card and extracted it from the soldier's hand. "Thank you officer, I'll try to remember that."

He gave him a contrived salute, as the barrier raised on its axis allowing him entry.

Driving through, he accepted the guidance of the military, pictorial signage, advising civilians to proceed with caution, and follow the painted white arrows, proudly pointing to different locations and buildings.

Parking alongside the 'Hangar' sign, he entered the immense 20,000 sq. ft. structure, and was confronted with row after row of folding chairs as far as the eye could see, and in the distance, he could make out a raised stage, with a huge, scaffolding canopy, abundantly littered with floodlights and wires, with large canvas curtains hanging off the ends of the structure, like the wings of a dove.

Walking down the narrow alleyway (between the chairs) leading to the stage area, he paused for a second, as he passed a large speaker cabinet mounted on a wide, steel support girder.

He thought to himself, *how can such a harmless object, like a speaker system, bring so much devastation to so many people?*

He omitted a deep sigh and carried on walking towards the front section of the hangar.

"Hi Brendan, how you hanging?" shouted Linda Ronstadt as he approached the stage. "Come round the back, I'll meet you there?"

Groping his way through the canvas drapes, Ronstadt came bounding towards him and lovingly draped her arms around his neck while placing a moist kiss on his unshaven cheek.

"Thank goodness you made it Brendan. I read about the attack on you in the local press and the indignities you suffered at the hands of the police? But now you're here, that's all that matters."

"Don't believe all you read Linda," said Cathel, as he flirtatiously squeezed her curvaceous backside!

She omitted a girlie squeak and nervously pulled away

from him, with a sly grin slowly erupting across her blushing face.

He gave her his best matinee idol smile? "Sorry about that Linda, but I couldn't resist it. I mean really, those tight pants you're wearing make your posterior look so inviting?"

"You cheeky son of a bitch," she uttered between smiling lips. "At least now I know the blow to your head didn't affect your shy demeanour?" She hysterically laughed, and gave him a peck again with her charming lips. "You're something else Brendan, totally dangerous but interesting? Now, let's get some singing done, shall we?"

He followed her closely up a flight of roughly formed steps leading to the stage area and no matter how he tried he could not retract his lustful eyes away from her magnificent gluteus maximus.

Well, she's definitely worth one, he inwardly murmured, before slapping himself on the side of his face for his debaucherous thoughts.

He was about to approach her again at the top of the stairs and inform her again of her feminine attributes, when he noticed General Tuzo heading across the stage in his direction. His rigid military hand outstretched towards him.

"Mr Flynn, so pleased to see you old chap. How's your wound? Well healed I hope?"

He clasped hold of the General's hand. "Yes, thank you, Sir. How's the show going?"

"Magnificently good Mr Flynn, thank you for asking. In fact, this show, I'm sure, is going to make a lot of depressed soldiers very happy. And don't forget old boy, there's only ten days to go before the big day." He eagerly grabbed hold of Cathel's elbow. "Isn't this exciting Brendan? But wait... I would like to introduce you to our first class sound man." He gesticulated towards a man on the periphery of the stage. "We were so very fortunate to have acquired such a talented, superb gentleman, and can you believe old chap, that he lives right here in Belfast. In fact, when you think about it, we have been so very lucky Brendan haven't we, and I truly feel…" He gave a visceral gaze at the roofing shell of the hangar. "I feel that somebody up there is really looking out for us in this endeavour."

Ya, right," said Cathel.

"No, no," replied the General, "I know you'll feel the same, once you've met this amazing, unassuming gentleman."

"Wow. I can't wait to meet him," said Cathel. His excitable expression instantly disappearing as soon as General Tuzo's back was turned.

They crossed the littered stage, with Cathel giving a wide birth to the speaker cabinets mounted on either side of the curtain support scaffold.

Walking to the centre of the stage, the General lightly tapped the shoulder of a man who was bent over meticulously threading black electrical cables through a small trapdoor, and he sprightly clambered to his feet and faced the two men.

Cathel found himself trying to assess the thin, wiry Irishman, whose sinewy face was almost concealed by a bushy red beard, seeming completely out of place on such a small insignificant man.

"Michael, I would like to introduce you to Brendan Flynn. Brendan, meet our electronics savour Michael Coburn."

The miniscule stature of a man held out his hand, and a deadly silence ensued before Cathel decided to shake it. Not once releasing his piecing blue eyes from Coburn's fidgety brown irises.

"Please to meet ya Brendan, and I know you're going

to be amazed at the progress we've made, especially with the sound system." He winked at Cathel. "And I'm certain this concert's going to be a blast." His eyes twinkled with delight, and Cathel quickly slid his hand away from Coburn's, as though he'd been touching something obscene and disgusting!

"So Coburn, I hear you're very good at what you do. Is that right?"

"You betcha Brendan," he said. "I must admit, I think I'm one of the best in my field, thanks to all the shows I've done for Rod Stewart and the Faces."

Cathel gave him a debilitating stare. "Rod Stewart? I've never heard of him." He turned to saunter away when General Tuzo forcefully grabbed hold of his sleeve and violently twisted him around.

"I say old chap," he announced, in his upper class tone. "I think that was rather rude of you if you don't mind me saying so. This gentleman Mr Flynn, has spent many hours making this sound system, impeccably perfect, in fact, I must say, he's spent far more hours preparing and working on this concert than he's ever been paid for, and I find that so admirable in this day and age. And I personally think you should actually show him the respect he certainly deserves."

Cathel raised his head and nodded in accord at Tuzo. His demeanour showing a festering helplessness?

"I'm sorry General, you are so right. I was just trying to be flippant. I apologise." He gave a 'boy scout salute' to Coburn. "See you Michael. Next time I'll try to treat you with the respect you deserve?" Brendan then gave Coburn, the same dubious glare that he'd received.

Linda Ronstadt came across and joined the threesome, and suggested to Cathel that they should walk to the officers' mess and discuss a few things. "But don't drink the tea, it's terrible," she whispered with a laugh as they exited.

They sat at one of the Formica topped, steel tables, that were scattered around the Anderson type mess hut. Its pastel green walls projecting an antiseptic clean atmosphere.

Two beers were served to the duo and they noisily clinked bottles.

"Cheers!" retorted Cathel.

"Brendan, why are you being such a prick?" she said. "I've noticed a change in you just lately, and it's beginning to piss me off…"

Cathel chugged on his beer, showing no sign of indifference. He placed the bottle on the faded Formica before addressing her. "Linda, what would it take to cancel this show?"

Showing complete shock, she ferociously stood, making the heavy metal chair she was seated on, fall backwards loudly, as it clattered upon the gleamingly polished, concrete painted floor. "What the hell are you saying Brendan?" She pointed her finger. "Don't you dare give me that superstar bullshit. I've met your type before!! You're bored with our rehearsals and suddenly, you, Mr Ego, thinks: Wait a minute, I could be doing something better with my time? Well bullshit! You pain in the arse actors are all alike. You don't give a damn about commitment. All you care about is your own vanity, and 'Bang' off you go. Well I'm telling you now Brendan, if you cancel out on this show, for whatever reason. I'll make sure that every newspaper and television corporation throughout the world, will blatantly broadcast how Mr Brendan Flynn, the famous philanthropic actor, known for his generous causes, cancelled a major concert for despondent army personal in Northern Ireland, who are fighting an enemy they cannot confront. Hence the enormous death rate of their comrades! Is that what you want Brendan?"

"Wow, hold your horses lady!" he shouted. "My name's not Bob Hope ya know? I don't make a living entertaining troops? I'm doing this concert because I was asked to do it, and I obliged. I only mentioned cancelling because I've been feeling some bad vibes about the concert. It's hard to explain Linda, but you know when you get that nervous feeling, deep down inside your lower stomach cavity as though something bad is going to happen, and you can't explain why? Well that's what I'm experiencing."

She smiled, and sitting back down, lovingly took hold of his hand. "Brendan," she said, "even Superstars get the jitters." She squeezed his hand compassionately. "You'll be okay on the night, trust me. But please, don't ever mention cancelling again, or otherwise, our sex may never happen?"

A look of surprise at her lascivious comment bespangled his brow. He broke free from her, to chugalug the rest of his beer, and then, interlocking his fingers once again with hers, said, "I'm so sorry Linda. I didn't mean to turn you into some kind of irate monster. I just thought, I'd try to explain what was bothering me." He let go of her slender fingers, hoping she couldn't sense the real frustrations bubbling inside of him.

She stood away from the table without drinking her beer. "Come on Bob," she mimicked, "we've got lots of rehearsals to get through."

Cathel stood, and started to sing 'Thanks for the memory' – Bob Hope's signature tune.

On entering back into the emptiness of the vast conscripted hangar, Cathel found himself fully immersed in the melodic music of the Horslips group who were now pounding out on stage, their innervated sound that had given a rebirth to crossover music for the youth of Ireland.

Grabbing the nearest folding chair, he sat and closed

his eyes, mentally absorbing the energy and musical talents of the Horslips rendition of 'Proud Mary' that vibrantly rattled throughout the ghostly structure of the converted hangar.

"What do ya think of the sound Brendan, pretty good eh?"

Cathel turned to his right, and observed Coburn standing in the middle row of chairs, eagerly turning knobs, and at the same time, meticulously moving a multitude of coloured levers (like the consummate professional that he was) as he adjusted the sound system through a large console board in front of him. Pressing a round, plastic disc on the complicated console, he locked in the achieved sound he then slid over and joined Cathel.

"Brendan," he whispered, "Can you believe we actually pulled this off?" He excitedly placed his sinewy hand on Cathel's folded arms. We'll be forever heroes in this blessed Country of ours?"

Cathel swiftly removed Coburn's hand, and sadly looked at Coburn. "Michael, I'd like you to dismantle the contraptions you've hidden inside the speaker boxes." Cathel inhaled deeply, visibly upset. "Coburn, instead of committing unprecedented mass murder, let's carry on with the methods we use now, and eventually the English will get disgruntled and leave, and the Brotherhood will then be remembered for their compassion and tolerance of this delicate situation that Northern Ireland now finds itself in, instead of being remembered for the genocidal mass murder that you and Adams are planning to perpetrate?"

Coburn vacated his chair. "Brendan, we are treated like aliens in our own country, but now this is our chance to show the bloody English that we're not the stupid 'Mick's' they think we are." He walked away from Brendan shaking his head in disbelief, as the last echo of 'Proud Mary' dissipated into the hangar rafters.

Cathel headed towards the stage area, lugubriously weighed down with an intensity of emotion as Linda sauntered over to greet him, her cheerful face beaming with delight until she saw his unsettled demeanour.

"Brendan whatever is wrong?"

"I need to talk to the General," he said.

She held on to him. "I'm sorry Brendan, you've just missed him, he left five minutes ago. But why…? Is there a problem?"

"No, no," he answered. "It's just important I to talk to him. I'll see ya tomorrow."

"What do you mean 'I'll see to you tomorrow'?" she screamed. "What about today's rehearsals? You egotistical bastard!"

Coburn ran to find the nearest telephone kiosk, as Cathel departed the Army complex with Ronstadt's obscenities still ringing in his ears.

Chapter 17

The Right Honourable Elizabeth Harley Crumley MP was too distraught to interact with the media as she left the Palace of Westminster after being denied the floor of the house once again? She had personally witnessed an incident in Northern Ireland, which she knew, was her right as a politician to bring to the attention of the House, but was consistently being denied. The subject she wanted to discuss with the sitting parliamentarians was not on the agenda for discussion, and therefore not allowed on the floor!!

The pompous, superior attitudes of her English colleagues, was the only thing she hated after becoming a politician, and she was completely amazed that anything of any importance was ever passed on the floor. Also, the irritable smell of twenty-year-old scotch, mingled with tinges of Madeira, incessantly drifting from every three pieced suited peerage seated in her vicinity forever stifled her intuitive thoughts.

Deciding to walk down the Mall towards the Trafalgar Hotel where she usually stayed while in London, she eventually cleared her mind of the day's events, turning as she did so to make sure her government vehicle was following close behind, and there it was - conspicuous by its presence.

She'd agreed the previous night to meet with a gentleman for a drink on her return to the hotel lounge. A complete sabbatical from her usual mind set, which consisted of very little variation while staying at the Trafalgar.

Elizabeth always enjoyed returning to the hotel after the repetitious performances in the house, and forever enjoyed the adulation bestowed on her by the staff of the Trafalgar who loved her dearly and showed it by catering too her every needs.

The staff knew she was still married to Brendan Flynn; the famous actor, and hoped one day they would all get to meet him if he ever walked in through the front entrance of the Trafalgar accompanying his wife for the 'unique' dinner that was specially prepared for her every night by the hotel's superlative chef: Consomme Soup; Mashed Potatoes; Grilled Brussels Sprouts; Well-done Beef; Bread and Butter Pudding to be served for dessert. No additions – no substitutes, but tonight would be different?

The previous night, after finishing her bread and butter pudding, and draining the last dregs of Asti Spumante from her glass, a stylishly dressed, incredibly handsome tall gentleman stopped at her table.

"Elizabeth Crumley?" he exclaimed.

"Who's asking?" she said.

He leaned over and cheekily smiled, as though bragging about his perfect set of sparkling white teeth. "Jack Hennessy, Republic of Ireland's new Ambassador to England at your service."

"Well pleased to meet you, Mr Hennessy," she said, as she stood to shake his hand. "But what happened to Ambassador O'Sullivan?"

He flashed his film star smile again. "Donal O'Sullivan had a few problems after President Nixon's visit, and eventually he was asked to resign and I'm glad to say I was offered the position, and if it's not too impertinent of me, do you mind if I join you?" He was extremely good looking and he knew it!

"Please," she answered, pointing to the chair opposite. Her heart started to palpitate! *What the hell am I doing?* she inwardly thought. *I don't do this type of thing. I hate all men, especially after Cathel's debaucherous treatment of me.*

He seated himself and smiled across at her, with Elizabeth trying to avoid the mischievous glint in his eyes. He opened his mouth to speak. "I was in the upper gallery today, and I was quite embarrassed watching those Jackals nibbling at you. But, as a fellow Irishman I would like to thank you for the wonderful support you give to our country, both north and south." He reached over to touch one of her delicate hands, which she quickly removed from the table

"Mr Hennessy, if you try to kiss my hand, I will surly hit you with this Asti bottle?"

He laughed loudly. She smiled.

"I understand," he said, thinking of how many times he'd read about her husband's hand kissing compulsion!! "Can we start this conversation again, Elizabeth, and I'll order another bottle of Asti. We can then sit here and I'll tell you how amazingly beautiful you are."

She laughed. 'You're so full of shit, Mr Hennessy."

"Thank you," he replied. "I just love your descriptive adjectives."

She smiled again.

"I'm sorry Mr Hennessy," she said, pushing herself away from the table, "but I've lots of phone calls to catch up with, and I'm going to practice my address once again, and hope it transpires to success on the floor tomorrow. So I'll say goodnight to ya." She rose from the table and Hennessy ran around and majestically helped to withdraw the chair she'd been sitting on.

"It was a pleasure Mrs Crumley," he mumbled, "and if you don't mind my bad manners, I'm staying in London 'til Friday, and with your permission I'd like to be seated at this table tomorrow night, at five pm precisely, with an open bottle of chilled Asti in anticipation of your arrival. Unless, of course, you give me that spit in the eye look again?"

Nervously, she looked into his dreamy eyes, and without a word, took hold of his hand (which smelled of Brut body wash), and raising it close to her open mouth, exaggerated a spitting sound directly into his open palm. She slowly closed his fingers around her fictional saliva, never once taking the look of intrigue, away from his handsome features.

"I'll see you tomorrow Mr Hennessy," she said. "And don't forget – no hand kissing?" She winked at him and walked towards the elevator.

Her hotel room was not luxurious, but comfortable, and on entering the room she kicked off her shoes in a nonchalant, devil may care way, and fell backwards like a Snow Angel on top of the puffy, floral bedspread that covered the four poster bed beneath her. She lay there, eyes wide open, with a wicked smile on her face.

A sexual tingle she'd thought long since extinguished, was now viciously creeping throughout her quivering loins as she conjured up the following nights indulgence.

"Christ!" she shouted at the top of her voice, the echo of it resonating around the room. "What the hell am I doing?"

She sprang off the queen-sized mattress, and gazing at her reflection in the bevelled wall mirror in front of her, grabbed a cigarette from a pack on the dresser, and lighting it, dangled it seductively from the corner of her mouth. She inhaled deeply, and blowing the smoke at her reflection, pretended to be Marlena Dietrich. She poised in what she thought was a seductive mode, and started to sing 'Falling in Love again' in an earthy sensual drawl, while still dangling the cigarette from her vivacious lips. Suddenly she laughed and laughed at her silliness, 'til tears rolled freely down her blushing cheeks.

On entering the Trafalgar, the next day, after another disgruntled performance on the floor of the house. She was approached by the hotel's aging concierge, who informed her that a gentleman visitor was waiting for her at her favourite table in the dining room.

Her heart started to flutter again as she rushed to the central elevator bank. She waited to ascend to her room, where her most expensive feminine clothing, (that she possessed) had been pressed and laid out for her, on top of the bedspread as per instructions.

Leisurely showering, in the hotels antiquated bathtub, with its enormous chrome taps that looked threateningly ugly. She provocatively soaped her lean athletic body longer than usual, until suddenly, the water pressure from the showerhead turned into a miniscule trickle, which quickly nudged her out of her self-induced trance.

Sitting naked in front of the kidney shaped dresser, Elizabeth attempted to brush out her tangled, limp hair, but after violently pulling at the knotted mess, threw the offending hair brush across the room!!

'To heck with it!" she screamed. "Who the hell is he anyway?"

She lit another cigarette and attempted to compose her reckless, nervous attitude, when it suddenly occurred to her that she knew nothing about this Jack Hennessy, and in fact, he could very well be a pain in the arse like all the rest of them.

"Fore Warned is Fore Armed," she said to herself, as she picked up the telephone receiver to dial the Irish Embassy on Grosvenor Place and talk to Molly Devlin, an attaché she remembered worked for the Embassy.

After being put on hold for what seemed like a life time, a crackling voice echoed from inside the earpiece. "Molly here."

"Molly," she answered, "Elizabeth Harley here. How you doing?"

'My god Elizabeth, I've not spoken to you in aeons, how have you been?"

"Listen Molly," she said, "I'm sorry but I don't have much time to talk so I'll come straight to the point? What is Jack Hennessy like?"

There was a moment of silence on the other end of the line. "Excuse me Elizabeth, but who the hell is Jack Hennessy?"

"Oh I'm sorry," she murmured, "I should have said Ambassador O'Sullivan's replacement, Ambassador Hennessy."

The same deadly silence ensued once again, with Molly Devlin eventually answering. "Elizabeth, I don't know what you've been drinking, or what you're on, but Ambassador O'Sullivan was never replaced, and in fact, he has just held a civic reception this afternoon for the Chinese delegation that President Nixon arranged before he left, and as for this Hennessy person, I have never heard of him."

Elizabeth slammed down the black receiver, without so much as a courteous goodbye.

She redressed in the clothes she'd worn all day at the parliament buildings. Catching a glimpse of herself and her messy hair in the hall mirror, she smirked and said to her reflection, "Amazingly beautiful eh, Mr Hennessy. Well wait to you get a load of this?"

He rose from his chair as she entered, and stood in polite anticipation of her joining him.

After shaking hands with the Maître d' she smiled and

160

walked over to Hennessy, thinking that the double breasted blue blazer he was wearing, looked completely out of place amongst all the dark suited, business gentry that were seated in his vicinity.

"Thank you Elizabeth," he said, "for accepting my invitation. You look lovely."

She smiled.

He pulled out a chair for her, and she sat down upon the red velvet cushion fastened to its base.

"So Mr Hennessy," she said, "I hope I didn't keep you waiting too long."

"It was worth the wait," came his reply, never once taking his eyes of her as he poured two glasses of Asti. They clinked glasses together. "Cheers," he said.

"Cheers," she answered, taking a sip of the refreshing drink. "Well Jack, what shall we talk about? Perhaps you can tell me what a typical day at the Embassy consists of, like today for instance, was anything interesting happening?"

He flashed his famous teeth. "Elizabeth, you can't believe how boring my days at the Embassy are, but enough about me, how was your day?"

She was about to release a barrage of derogatory insults towards him, when the immaculately dressed waiter came to their table.

"Good evening Mrs Crumley, will it be two for your special dinner tonight?"

She removed a cigarette from an Embassy packet and smiled as the waiter produced a Bic lighter from his apron pocket and held its flickering yellow flame beneath her cigarette, after she'd placed it between her lips.

"Good evening to you also, Joseph," she announced, through a haze of second hand smoke. "I'm afraid Mr Hennessy will not be staying for dinner?"

"Of course Mrs Crumley," he replied.

Jack Hennessy rubbed his pouting lips with agitated fingers? "Excuse me, Elizabeth," he exclaimed, "but I thought we'd be dining together tonight?"

She viciously crushed her cigarette into a cut glass ashtray on the table, and gave him a distasteful frown. "Well, we might have been perhaps twenty minutes ago Mr fuckin Jack Hennessy." She lit another cigarette and studied his expression. "That is, until I had a little conversation with a friend of mine who works at the Irish Embassy. So tell me Jack. When did you say Ambassador O'Sullivan resigned?"

His body language said it all as she looked at his fidgeting hands, clasped on the table in front of him.

He cast a sorrowful gaze across at Elizabeth. "I'm sorry about that Elizabeth, it was just a little white lie." He breathed deeply as he tried to appease her. "I couldn't believe it was you sat there yesterday, and I've admired and respected you for a long, long time, but I knew I wouldn't get to first base with you unless I came up with some sort of commonality between us. So I came up with the Ambassador ploy. And let's face it Elizabeth, it worked for a while?" He now felt more relaxed and flashed his white teeth smile at her again. "So there you have it Elizabeth. I'm so happy to be talking to you and being allowed to be sharing the same table and if you can find it in yourself to forgive me, I'm sure we can carry on where we left off and have a wonderful night together?"

She had another sip of her Asti. "Well Mr Hennessy," she replied, "you've got one thing right, you certainly wouldn't have got to first base with me, and in fact the ball you attempted to hit to first base has just landed in the catcher's mitt, and that means you're out. Good night Jack."

He tried to grab her hand, and she venomously glared

at him.

"Now Jack, you see those two gentlemen standing at the entrance of the restaurant. Well, they are commonly referred to as plain clothed police officers from Scotland Yard, whose job it is to protect government officials like me from stalkers, like you Jack!" And by the way, they are armed! And one hand signal from me and you will be arrested, okay?"

Hennessy's eyes seemed to cloud over. He stood and leaned across the table. "Armed you say Elizabeth? Well that's funny because so am I."

She gave a trembling deep sigh as he walked round to her side of the table and unbuttoning his double breasted blazer, exhibited to her a shabby, brown shoulder holster tightly strapped to his impressive chest.

She waited for the contaminated panic she felt to surge throughout the busy dining room, but realised it was just self-indulgence, and the same mood of total oblivion to her situation had not interfered with any of the other restaurant patrons.

He swiftly grabbed hold of her trembling hand before she could resist, and raising it to his lips, kissed the back of it! "Well thank you, Elizabeth," he said, as he re-buttoned his jacket. "I'm sure you don't want me to start anymore trouble in this favourite hotel of yours than I already have done, and it would be such a shame to see this charming establishment closed down for a week or two, because of some outrageous shootout that occurred here?" He smirked at her "You see Elizabeth, I'm also not on my own, and have what you would call 'back-up'. So I'll say goodnight to ya. It's been a most enlightening experience and I'm sure we could have had a wonderful meal together, and who knows, maybe later we could have had...? Anyhow, give my regards to your husband, and please inform him how easy it was for me to penetrate your so-called security."

"My dammed husband!" she yelled. 'What the hell has he got to do with anything?"

Hennessy bent over, alarming close to her face. "Just tell Mr Brendan Flynn that he'd better do as we ask, or things could get ugly? So once again Elizabeth, it's been a pleasure, and please don't mention this conversation to anyone, except your husband of course, or otherwise Mr Flynn's career could dramatically be shortened somewhat?"

He turned and walked away from her, menacingly grinning at the plain clothed officers as he left the restaurant.

Chapter 18

Cathel half opened his eyes, and reaching out from under the bedsheets, grabbed the incessantly ringing telephone.

"Cathel, is that you?"

He sat bolt upright on recognising Elizabeth's voice. She never phoned!!

"Hi ya doing?" he answered, in a low obsequious tone.

"How am I doing!" she exclaimed. "Well I'd be doing a lot better if my 'ex-husband' didn't keep getting me involved in his disgusting life. Get out here now, you stupid man!"

"Yes madam," he replied. "But do you mind if I have a shower first?"

The line went 'Dead'.

After showering, he grabbed a slice of bread from his depleted fridge, and covering it with Pork drippings and a generous amount of salt, ran from the house as he bit into his gourmet creation!

She was waiting under the dreary Gargoyles, at the rear entrance of the Priory, in a defiant stance, her arms tightly folded in anticipation!

Cathel sped down the driveway, and seeing her seething bodily deportment, purposely accelerated his MG. Then abruptly turning the steering wheel, proceeded to perform screaming 'doughnuts' in front of her, sending gravel and dust particles in all directions.

"That just about sums you up!" she shouted, trying hard

to be heard over the mayhem he was creating.

"What's wrong princess?" he shouted back. "What happened to your sense of humour? It's called having fun."

She walked over to the little car, and reaching in, grabbed his shirt collar. "I hope you also think this is fun Cathel, when I tell you about this 'man' who invaded my privacy at the Trafalgar by false pretences, and then suggested I tell my husband how easy it was to bypass my government security. Do you find that funny Cathel? Especially when he politely informed me, and showed me, that he was armed!!" She prodded her finger, time after time into his chest. "Do you realise I had to take a government emergency flight out of London last night just to sort this shit out. So Cathel!" she screamed. "What the fuck have you got us involved in now?"

Cathel's face turned a ghostly shade as he slowly turned off the ignition. He then sat vacantly staring through the front windshield, seemingly void of all emotion.

Elizabeth swore under her breath and started to walk towards the Priory rear entrance when suddenly she was roughly spun around.

Cathel then released his hold on her, as she stood and faced him.

"Elizabeth," he murmured. I'll try and explain if you'd give me half a chance?"

She viciously slapped him across the face. "You bastard!" she screamed. "When the hell are you going to get out of my life? You swagger around as though you're King Shit, but what are you really Cathel? Well I'll tell you what you are, you're nothing!" She slapped him again and he clenched his fist. "Do you hear me Cathel Crumley, you're nothing. You're an IRA sympathiser who supports a terrorist organisation that's destroying this bloody country of ours?" She glared at him with a vindictive fervour that punctuated her every word as they expectorated themselves from her truculent mouth. "When are you stupid people going to realise that violence achieves nothing – get used to it Cathel. This is as good as it gets, and for God's sake, try to enjoy your country for what it is." She suddenly burst into tears.

"Listen, will ya?" he shouted. "You're right, violence achieves nothing. That's why you were approached by the man at the Trafalgar. I was asked by the Brotherhood to participate in a scheme which involved considerable violence and carnage against the British, and I refused. I've tried to explain to them that there are other ways to achieve independence in Northern Ireland without bloodshed, but they won't listen."

He held onto her, and lost himself into her tear filled pupils, and raising his left hand, gently stroked the side of her face, as a crescendo of moisture started to cloud his own vision.

She looked up at him as he spoke.

"Elizabeth. I promise you, I'll sort this out and nobody will ever molest you again. My association with the IRA is over, and from now on, they can collect their own bloody Noraid donations." He held her hand. "But Elizabeth, I will always be Catholic, and I will always fight for Northern Ireland's independence by any other means but violence."

He wiped the tears from his eyes, and then turning, walked towards his car.

The armour plated, white, RUC Land Rover, roared down the driveway of the Priory. Its blue lights flashing wildly as Cathel was about to climb into his MG. It came to an abrupt stop a few yards away from Elizabeth and two uniformed officers ran from the vehicle towards her.

"Sorry for the intrusion madam," said one of the officers. "But you must accompany us immediately!"

She gave him a look of total disbelief. "What? Why? What is this all about?"

"I'm sorry to inform you madam," said the officer as he looked for conformation from his colleague, "but there's been a kidnapping from outside of your son's school, and we've been asked to drive and accompany you there."

"Oh God no!" she screamed, as she lugubriously clasped her hands to her face. "Not Patrick!!"

The thirty-minute drive to the Royal Private School in Dungannon was accompanied by a deadly silence as Elizabeth and Cathel sat uncomfortably crammed on the rear seats of the police Land Rover.

The first thing that alarmed them as they stepped from the vehicle, was the abundance of RUC vehicles parked alongside the curb at the side of the school. They intentionally blocked the whole length of Ranfury Road with blue uniformed officers positioned in all directions. Transforming the otherwise tranquil environment of Dungannon, into a simulated war zone!

A senior officer with a row of shiny pips extending from his shoulder epaulets, rushed over to acknowledge the famous duo. When suddenly Elizabeth started to scream at the top of her lungs?

There, parked between the procession of yellow decaled police vehicles, was her father's black Daimler limousine. The right side of the car completely shrouded in a large, white cloth, which also obscured the open aperture of the driver's door.

She started to run towards the Daimler when a plain clothed officer appeared, and gently grabbed hold of her before she reached the limousine. "Sorry madam," he said, "but you don't want to get any closer than this. The white sheet is covering the body of your father's chauffeur who was gunned down while trying to stop the kidnapping of your son." He looked down. "And I'm sorry, it's not a pretty sight."

Elizabeth's eyes rolled into the back of her head as she collapsed towards the pavement, with the plain clothed officer catching her before she hit the ground.

Cathel stood completely exasperated as he surveyed the scene unfolding in front of him when he recognised Major Pedigrew Jennings in the distance. He was with an officious looking group of gentlemen, and on seeing Cathel excused himself and headed towards him.

He held out his hand and Cathel limply grasped hold of it.

"Sorry about this Brendan old chap, but we both knew something like this was bound to happen after what happened to Francis?"

Cathel breathed in deeply, visually disturbed. "Who? I mean what the hell? Why Major?"

Pedigrew intuitively rolled the piece of paper he held in his hand, before answering. "Well Brendan, as far as we can assess, Sir Charles Harley's chauffeur was sat waiting in the Daimler where you can see it parked…" he pointed to the curb, "for your son to come out of the front entrance of the school. And when the bell rang, allowing the boys to exit the building, your son walked towards the limousine, like he usually did, when two foreign looking men, who'd also been sat in a vehicle parked at the curb, jumped out and attempted to drag your son to their car. The chauffeur on observing this, opened the glove box of the Daimler and withdrew a concealed weapon. He then slowly opened the driver's door and pointed an army issue revolver at the would-be kidnappers. Unfortunately, the third member of the trio – who'd been hiding behind the limousine – saw what was happening, and creeping down the side of the Daimler, shot the chauffeur point blank in the side of the head."

Cathel thought for a moment before asking Pedigrew, "What sort of car were they in?"

The major, gauging Cathel's demeanour, looked down at the piece of paper in his hand and reading it aloud said: "A maroon Humber Super Snipe." He carried on talking as he noticed the surprise look on Cathel's face. "Nobody noted the licence plate number I'm afraid. They just watched, petrified to the spot, as your son was bungled in the rear seat of the Humber, and it hurriedly took off along Ranfurly Road, and at the bottom crossroads, turned left." Pedigrew took hold of Cathel's shoulders and gave him a sympathetic hug. "Don't worry old chap," he said. "We have an all-points bulletin out on the Humber, and every police officer within a twenty-mile radius will be on alert 'til we find it."

"Forget about your all-points bulletin. Do you have any well-armed men with you?"

Pedigrew looked completely bemused. "Of course I do, Brendan old chap, but why?"

"Because I know where they've taken him. Let's go!" he excitedly shouted.

The white Ford Escort sped along the A50 on Cathel's directions, with the three other occupants appearing pensive and stern.

"Okay," shouted Cathel. "At the third roundabout turn right onto Lurgan Road, and then turn left on Ballybrick."

Pedigrew nodded his head in acknowledgement, while Cathel annoyingly banged the flat of his hand on the dash pad, as though urging the vehicle to go faster.

At the end of Ballybrick, the Escort turned onto Murray's Hollow's.

"Now, now!" shouted Cathel. "Turn left onto Seafin Lane." Nervous excitement could be heard in Cathel's voice, as he started to stammer. "We, we could go down to the bottom of Murray's Hollow's, and it's a lot quicker, but I'm sure they'd see us comin'. Suddenly he screamed, "Stop!" as they came upon Randle's Farm.

The car skidded to a halt, unsettling most of the agents. He turned his head towards them.

"This is where you'll be needing your guns me thinks."

Pedigrew pulled up the handbrake and slid his face sideways to meet Cathel's stare. "Okay Brendan," he muttered. "Now I think the time is right, to explain to us what the hell is this all about, old chap?"

Ignoring him, he opened the car door and stepping out, slowly gazed across the valley towards the mist covered Slemish Mountain range as though he'd never laid eyes on them before. He then emptied a Park Drive from its packet, and placed it between his lips, and after lighting it with a match, inhaled deeply.

Pedigrew walking around from the other side of the vehicle, and removing a Senior Service from his gold cigarette case, reciprocated the actions of Cathel. The smoke from which mingled with Cathel's outward breath as he spoke. "Major, twenty minutes' drive down this lane, you'll come across an abandoned dairy farm that is being used by our infamous Libyan mercenaries. They've converted it into their make shift headquarters." He spat a loose tobacco strand from his teeth and grimmist. "And guess what kind of vehicle they drive? A Humber Super Snipe."

Pedigrew omitted a low growling whistle as he stubbed his cigarette out with one of his highly polished, brown brogues.

Fifteen minutes later the Major once again brought the Escort to a grinding halt as the lane became completely engulfed, in smog like thick smoke!!

"Where the heck is all this smoke coming from?" he

uttered.

Cathel leaned out of the open side window of the Escort and gazed down the lane.

Smoke was rapidly billowing out of a lower field, in the direction of their final destination.

He sadly looked back at Pedigrew with a dejected scowl, who knowingly, rammed the vehicle into gear and sped blindly through the smoke haze blanketing the lane, as they raced towards the dairy.

Two Green Goddess fire tenders blocked their way as they attempted to gain access into the farmyard. One tender, was busily trying to douse flames leaping out of the abandoned farmhouse roof, while the other tender was watering down, what remained of a large burned out carcass of a Humber Super Snipe!!

Pedigrew wound down the door glass and flashed his ID at a high ranking fire chief who stood surveying the scene. "Any fatalities chief?" he shouted.

"Don't think so," he quickly answered. 'We did a thorough search when we first arrived. We could still gain access to the farmhouse at that time, and everything seemed deserted. We also searched the two outbuildings which were still smouldering, but the floors were empty, apart from fire debris."

The major thanked him and wound the door glass back into place.

"I don't understand," said Cathel, "why would they set fire to everything?"

Pedigrew hesitated for a moment, then lit another cigarette. "Brendan, do you remember the Great Train Robbery in England in 1963?"

Cathel shrugged his shoulders. "Of course, but what's that got to do with anything?"

Pedigrew expelled the cigarette smoke from his mouth.

"Well I'll tell you Brendan old chap. The only reason we caught all those baddies so quickly, was because one of the gang namely Gordon Goody, paid a certain gentleman ten thousand pounds to burn down Leatherslade Farm, when all the members of the gang, and their thirty bags of money had vacated the building! You see Brendan, they'd been hiding there after the robbery, and they knew that if the police found out about the farm, they'd search it for fingerprints and other incriminating evidence. Unfortunately, the man that Goody paid the money too, to destroy the farm. Absconded with the ten thousand pounds to Marbella in Spain, leaving the intact Leatherslade a treasure trove of forensic evidence for the police and my department to sift through, especially all the fingerprints on the Monopoly game that most members of the gang had been playing with – hence all the speedy arrests. So Brendan, do you see why the Libyans, and whoever else frequented these buildings, burned it to the ground?"

Cathel jumped from the Escort, his haunting screams rustling through the leaves of the tall Elms surrounding the farmyard.

On his return to the Priory with Pedigrew, they were greeted by two armed police officers at the rear entrance.

Cathel thanked the Major for the ride, and looking a little worse for wear, strolled towards the officers to gain entry to Elizabeth's study.

"Sorry, sir," said one of the policemen, "but we're here to inform you that you are no longer welcome at this establishment, and an emergency restraint warrant has been granted, ordering you not to approach, or to come within five hundred yards of this building, otherwise you will be arrested for harassment and trespassing. Do you understand, sir?"

"Fuck you!" shouted Cathel, as he attempted to force

his way through, between the burly officers, where he was roughly grappled to the gravel and handcuffed, while still hurling insults at his aggressors.

The centuries old door of the Priory flew open, and the imposing figure of Sir Charles blocked the entrance. His outline ghostly illuminated by the effulgent of light being omitted from the hallway.

He reached out and slapped Cathel ferociously across the face, while the officers attempted to control him as he violently struggled between them. Sir Charles, tightly squeezed Cathel's chin, with his thumb and forefinger, and grossly spat in his face! "Now listen to me, you disgusting piece of shit – you know I've never liked you, and you damn well know why. Because, in my opinion, you're the lowest of the lowest, you have no breeding, and no manners, and thank god, my daughter now realises this. You have brought nothing but disgrace to my family name. So, I'm going to tell you this, Mr Brendan Flynn, or whatever your stupid name is, if anything should happen to my grandson, I will personally hold you responsible, and you'll suffer the same consequences! Do you understand? And if you ever venture on these grounds again, I will have you shot for trespassing."

He then addressed the policemen.

"Now gentlemen, will you please remove this slime off my doorstep." He then withdrew, and slammed the heavy robust door of the Priory.

After removing the handcuffs, he was roughly manhandled and pushed into the driver's seat of his MG and asked to leave.

Switching on the ignition, he slowly turned the steering wheel and headed down the driveway.

"Nice to see you, sir," shouted one of the officers, with his next obtrusive comments being completely drowned out by their laughter.

Cathel sped down the gravel drive towards the marble Lions on the periphery of the estate, while mentally dissecting the circumstances he found himself in.

Eventually reaching his secluded cottage, he hastily opened the front door and entering in, collapsed, exhausted, on the nearest couch.

Twenty minutes later, he was awaked from his slumber, by his monotonous phone again. Answering it, he omitted a groaning, "What?"

"As-Salaam Alaikum, Ustaaz Flynn, how is you?"

Cathel sprang off the couch as though stung by a Bee!

"Yahmed!" he screamed. "Where's my boy – you son of a bitch!"

"Oh, I get yours attention yes?" he replied.

"Listen you Libyan fuckhead! If you harm my son, I will tear you apart, limb from limb."

"Oh, you so tough Mr actor man. You make a me shake." The general's hearty laugh, could be heard vibrating down the phone. "You use mouth too much actor man, now listen to me for change. You sing, one week from now in hangar and get son back, okay?"

Cathel held the phone tightly to his ear as his hand began to shake wildly, in response to the convulsive, tonic spasms overtaking his body. "Okay, okay... I'll do it, but please don't hurt him."

"No problem Ustaaz Flynn. Why would I hurt such beautiful boy? I tell you Flynn, your son look younger than nine, now that he naked beside me!!

Tears streamed down Cathel's cheeks from sheer frustration, and an apocalyptic whisper escaped from his throat!! "General, if you touch my son in any way, I will find you, no matter how long it takes, you perverted bastard!"

Yahmed laughed. "Yes, yes, I hear you. Do you wish

175

blow him kiss down phone, then? I promise, I give to him, along with my own affections?"

The expletive obscenities pouring from Cathel's mouth, were wasted on the disconnected phone line!!

Chapter 19

It had been a worrisome and frustrating week for Cathel, since his son had been kidnapped. Unbeknown to him, his phone in the cottage had been bugged by MI5, and as soon as the lewd, debaucherous conversation he'd listened to from Yahmed was over, Pedigrew had walked into his cottage unannounced, and politely explained about the phone tap. Cathel had viciously torn into him, ranting and raving about privacy laws and a person's rights, until suddenly he succumbed to his attritional grief, and became a depleted, crestfallen soul in front of the Major.

Eventually, feeling the relief to be sharing his knowledge of the horrific plot to destroy the Thiepval hangar with someone else he relaxed, with Pedigrew thanking him for divulging the information.

"Now Brendan, let's work out how we're going to deal with this situation?"

Rehearsals carried on as normal so's not to arouse suspicion, especially with Michael Coburn, who seemed to be watching Cathel's every move.

Cathel adopted a conciliatory attitude towards everyone, especially to Coburn whenever possible, and had even informed him that the BBC were sending an outside broadcasting team to film the entire concert, at which Coburn had shook his clenched fist in the air, and shouted a resounding "Yes" as he explained to Cathel in his macabre way, that all the world would now see 'how' in his own words: "How we get rid of our English aggressors." He then gave Cathel a high five.

Linda Ronstadt had also commented on his new demeanour by saying, "I'd like to welcome the 'Old Brendan' back to us, it's a pleasure to see you."

Lieutenant General Harry Tuzo, was sworn to secrecy, and was now treating the whole scenario like a military exercise (of which he was renowned for), explaining to his subordinate officers the logistics of moving hundreds of army personal and having as many ambulances on standby that he could muster to complete the illusion of mass injuries and deaths, on the night of the concert. He strongly relayed to everyone present; at his covert, strategy and tactics meeting, the importance of secrecy, forever quoting Second World War statements made by Winston Churchill: "Remember gentlemen, 'Walls have ears', and 'Loose lips sink ships'."

The classy, Atkinson tractor trailer ensemble steadily drove along Ormeau Road, with large black decals, plastered on the sides of the trailer, blatantly advertising BBC OUTSIDE BROADCASTING. It eventually stopped alongside the Havelock House Television Studios after the long trip of being loaded on the car ferry at the Holyhead, Scottish ferry terminal, and then, after crossing the rough Irish Sea, had been unloaded at the Belfast ferry terminal.

Derek Meddings, and the other four members of the special effects team, alighted the vehicle and entered the studios that Cathel had entered a few hours before, and after being ushered into the sound studio situated in the basement of the building, Cathel greeted Meddings with a meaningful handshake.

"Great to see you again Derek, and congratulations on your new Bond movie, I hear the special effects are incredible, and I love the title *Live and Let Live*, quite a catchy title, eh Derek?"

Meddings nodded. "Nice to see you also Brendan, but what's all this cloak and dagger stuff? I was just about to leave on a belated holiday with my wife to Jamaica, when I was approached by the head of Shepperton Studios, and politely asked if I would mind taking all the pyrotechnics, and special effects equipment we had used on the Bond movies, and head to Northern Ireland to meet you. And the worst part Brendan, is that I wasn't allowed to even tell my wife where I was going! So what's it all about Brendan?"

Pedigrew stood and walked over to Meddings. "Excuse me sir, but I would like to introduce myself." He removed his identity wallet from his inside pocket and opened it for Meddings to read. "My name sir, is Major Pedigrew Jennings, and I work for her Majesty's Security Service – MI5."

"Bloody hell!" uttered Meddings. He attempted to make an admonitory gesture, but Pedigrew interjected.

"Mr Meddings, what you're now going to hear is an outline of a plan that we would like you and your crew of pyrotechnics, to perform for us with the uppermost of secrecy. Mr Flynn here, is already involved, and because of his previous actions in regards to this matter, he has already saved more British Army lives, than were ever lost on the Normandy beaches in the last war."

"Wow! Well excuse me," said Meddings, deep in thought. "So you're saying this is dangerous?"

"Only if you, or one of your technicians, lights the wrong fuse."

Pedigrew sniggered and lit a cigarette. "Gentlemen, we need your expertise you've used for years in the movies. And now we need you to use that knowledge to save real lives, okay?"

Meddings looked at Cathel. "Is this for real Brendan, or

is this another of your famous pranks? Remember, I know you very well, and I've been caught out with your silly hoaxes before."

Cathel sighed. "Derek, this is so for real, and I think when this is over, you may even receive the OBE from Pedigrew's bosses?"

"Gentlemen!" screamed Pedigrew. "Can we proceed? Mr Meddings, three days from now, we hope that you and your team can simulate an explosion of unprecedented proportions on the roof of a converted aircraft hangar at the Thiepval Army Barracks here in Belfast. It must appear to onlookers, that sixteen pounds of Semtex plastic explosive, has just been detonated. Is that possible?"

"Anything's possible," he answered.

"Possible!" exclaimed Joe Hurst, one of the other technicians. "Do you realise what damage sixteen pounds of 'PETN' can do?"

"Excuse me, but what is PETN?" asked Pedigrew scratching his head.

Meddings laughed. "Sorry about Joe, sir. He's the chemist amongst us, and he always abbreviates things. He means the main component of Semtex is Pentaerythritol-Tetranitrate, in short, 'PETN'. And he's right, that amount of Semtex could bring a whole building down."

Pedigrew gesticulated. "That's the point. That's what you have to simulate, but we would ask that corresponding collateral damage be kept to a minimum with regards to buildings and homes in the vicinity. Your explosions should occur at exactly twenty hundred hours on Saturday night. The same time the supposed concert was planned to start."

"Concert, what concert?" asked Meddings.

"Never mind, never mind," said the irritable Major. "You and your team will drive directly from here to the

Thiepval Barracks. There you'll be met by General Tuzo who will be waiting for you, and once inside the confines of the camp, you should unload the cameras and lighting equipment that Michael Swann, the chairman of the board of the BBC has kindly loaned us."

"Blimey!" sighed Meddings. "You certainly know people at the top don't you? First I'm approached by Flanders, the head of Shepperton, and now I'm borrowing equipment from the head of the BBC. Christ! How do you know all these people?"

"That does not concern you, can we proceed please," said Pedigrew. "Now, don't worry about those cameras, you don't have to know how they function, because they are what you call in the movie industry, 'Props'. They are plastered in BBC signage decals, and that's your cover for being there. Alas, we do have one thorn in our side, namely Michael Coburn, who will now be referred to as the enemy? This gentleman on arrival at Thiepval tomorrow morning, will be sent on a wild goose chase, on pretence that more equipment is needed for the show."

"What show?" guffawed Meddings.

Pedigrew ignored him. "Gentlemen, I must stress once again, that no way can you arouse the suspicions of Coburn, and if by chance you come across him, please act normal. We have made sure that he'll be away for most of the day tomorrow, and that's when you little beavers will get to work!! You will receive further instructions from General Tuzo, on arrival at the barracks, so good luck."

"Crikey, these people are something else," uttered Meddings to the rest of his bemused crew, as they were led from the room.

Cathel dug into his cigarette packet and offered the Major a Park Drive.

"I'm sorry," he said, "but no thanks – I have an allergy against smoking horse manure!!" He pretended to convulse, and then removed a Senior Service from his gold cigarette case, and releasing a satisfactory sigh, inhaled the blue smoke after lighting it.

Suddenly the atmospheric mood between the two, changed.

"Okay, Major Pedigrew Jennings, where's my son?" screamed Cathel. "You promised me that you'd track the Libyans down in no time at all, but all you seem to be doing now, is avoiding the issue. So where is he, for God's sake?"

Pedigrew stood there with a dejected look on his face. Then, placing his hand on Cathel's forearm, gave it a comforting squeeze.

"I know you're frustrated old chap, and I apologise. We have high ranking, counter-espionage army officers, mixed in with MI5 intelligent agents and communication specialists, diligently bent over listening devices. All of them, irritatingly cramped around the small table in your cottage, just waiting for a break, and trust me Brendan, we're almost there. The search area has been narrowed down to within a twenty-mile radius of the city. And we have now bugged every public phone at the army base, as we feel that it's only a matter of time before that Coburn character attempts to contact them. Then we'll have a recorded trace and that will be the end of this. Just remember Brendan, I'm getting it from all sides? Sir Charles Harley is pulling strings all the way to Downing Street, and your wife telephones my office every day, either sobbing or shouting innuendoes about going to the press. Which of course, would be the worst thing she could possibly do? We need to keep this under wraps, so as not to alarm anyone into doing anything drastic. They must not find out the agency is involved. That's why we've not arrested Adam's. We've had him under surveillance for some time, but so far, he has not contacted anyone of any importance. And if we'd approached him, it could have blown up in our faces – if you'll excuse the expression!!"

"Well aren't you funny, you smug bastard!" exclaimed Cathel.

"I'm smug?" answered Pedigrew. "Don't forget who your wife's family blames for everything that's happening, Mr Brendan Flynn. So please don't try to put the onus on me, there's a good chap. It will only make things worse."

Cathel glared at him and walked away.

The tractor trailer unit was directed to the parking area made ready for it at the side of the hangar, the BBC equipment was methodically unloaded by a platoon of privates.

Meddings was still conferring with Tuzo, when he felt a tap on his shoulder.

"Derek Meddings, is that you?"

He turned around. "Excuse me, but do I know you?"

"Of course you do. Don't you remember? My name is Michael Coburn and we met earlier in the year at the Abbey Lane recording studios, where Pink Floyd and their managers were trying their uppermost to persuade you to do the pyrotechnics, for the groups up and coming DARK SIDE OF THE MOON TOUR and I was there because I'd been recommended by Rod Stewart to do their acoustics."

Meddings looked shocked, but rapidly regained his composure. "Of course, now I remember. How are you, Mr Coburn?"

"Please call me Michael," he said. "But why are you here with a BBC outside broadcast team. I thought all you did was pyrotechnics?"

Meddings noticed the General had adopted a wide eyed, nervous stance, as though he was expecting a full frontal attack, and he smiled across at him. "Is it okay if I tell him, sir?"

The General's eyes seemed to widen even more, as he blurted out. "It's entirely up to you."

Meddings addressed Coburn. "Well, if you can keep a secret Michael, after the concert, the General thought his men would love to see a spectacular fireworks display. And I readily agreed to be available to perform this."

General Tuzo removed his cap, and wiped his brow. "Bloody malaria," he said, after nervously looking at Meddings.

"Excellent idea!" exclaimed Coburn, although he was thinking, don't worry about fireworks General, there'll be enough before the concert.

Coburn put out his hand and the General grabbed hold of it. "What a wonderful idea, General. You're such a caring man, and I can't wait to see the end result! And Derek, if I can assist you in any way, like with the wiring or anything, just let me know."

"Bloody hell!" said the General, as he wiped his brow once again, when Coburn eventually sauntered away.

Chapter 20

The tension on the day of the supposed concert was electric, to say the least.

Michael Coburn had been arrested the day previous, as he attempted to leave the red telephone kiosk on the base, where MI5 agents were diligently trying to trace the number of the call that he had just made to General Yahmed, informing him that everything was going according to plan. The reason his arrest was activated, was because halfway through the conversation that was being recorded, Yahmed informed him not to try and make contact again until after the explosion!

Pedigrew acted swiftly and arrested Coburn as he vacated the kiosk, knowing that to remove him immediately from the base would in no way arouse suspicion, as his contact with General Yahmed had now been severed.

After five hours of interrogation by army intelligence. Coburn had revealed the telephone number he'd been given, to enable him to make contact with the Libyans.

But alas the phone line had been disconnected by the time they'd gleaned the information.

MI5 had eventually tracked down the registered address of the number, from the local phone company, and the cottage was now under surveillance, although the reports coming back to Pedigrew, hinted that no sign of life seemed to be present (in or around the building) A small force of civilian clothed SAS officers were now discreetly on standby in the area, just in case any sort of premeditated procedure by the elite squad members, alerted the kidnappers of British Army presence.

Chapter 21

The massive explosion and subsequent fireballs, illuminated the overcast night sky over Belfast, giving it a surreal, translucent glow, that could be seen in outlying districts, and fifteen minutes after the pandemonium created by the blast, access roads and connecting arteries leading to the Thiepval Army Barracks were in lock-down mode. The only vehicles being allowed entry were Fire Department personnel, and an incessant stream of ambulances – all timed to perfection like the opening night of a Broadway theatre performance.

Cathel's last phone call from Yahmed, came two hours before commencement of the fictitious show, informing him that his son would be dropped off at the Priory, just as soon as he received confirmation of the explosion.

Desperately hiding his repulsive aversion towards the General, and knowing that God only knew how many people were listening to their conversation, he tried to keep talking as long as possible, by asking pertinent questions about his son's well-being, and how he had doubts to whether he could still trust the General's word on his son's release?

Yahmed, totally ignoring Cathel's rantings, finally said, "Have nice day actor man." He then slammed down the receiver.

Cathel still pensively sat at the side of his phone an hour later, internally debating to himself as to whether he could have better handled the situation, with regards to the Libyans!

"Perhaps," he said to the inner Cathel Crumley, "I should have informed the authorities as soon as General Melud Ali Yahmed had raised his ugly head, on that regrettable morning, on the way to Newcastle."

Then, ten minutes before the original concert was timed to commence, his telephone rang!

"Okay Brendan," said the whispering voice of Pedigrew on the end of the line. "We've found them. We traced the General's last call, and we are now surrounding the building. Here's the address…"

At exactly 20:00 hours, the warped door of the dilapidated building, creaked open on its rusted hinges, and Major Salah Dun Halasa, stepped out into the chilly night air, and placing a cigarette between his lips, silently gazed across towards the sound of the 'impressive' explosion, and the unnatural colour of the bloodshot night sky above Belfast. He smiled with satisfaction and withdrew a lighter from his trouser pocket, but the sniper's bullet ricocheted through his rib cage before he had chance to partake in the indulgence of a 'smoke'. He noiselessly collapsed, into a depleted human heap.

Six, black clad SAS commandoes burst into the building, followed closely by Pedigrew and a MI5 associate.

"All clear!" shouted the lead officer, after a few bursts of gunfire.

Pedigrew, swiftly ran down a dark inside passageway, situated on the second floor landing of the building. Taking care as he did so, not to trip over the body of a large, well-built man, who lay face down on the dirty, upstairs landing floor. Blood could be seen oozing out of the scorched gaping holes in the back of his bullet riddled shirt.

On reaching the open doorway, guarded by the lead soldier, he looked inside. There, lying naked on a soiled mattress in the middle of the empty room, lay General Yahmed, a crumpled bedsheet was strategically covering his genitals.

The sickening, solicitous smile on his face, looked completely out of place, with regards to the circumstances he found himself in.

Pedigrew heard a faint sobbing noise and turning, saw in the damp corner of the room, a young naked boy, curled up in the foetus position.

Pedigrew slowly walked over and held out his hand to assist the terrified boy, who, on his approach towards him, screamed. "No! No! Please, no!"

Pedigrew felt sick to his stomach when he noticed festering cigarette burns, blistering ferociously, across the boy's upper body.

He turned back towards the General. "You are disgusting, sir! You're a fucking, poor imitation of a man!" He angrily breathed deeply. "I thought, sir, that I had observed every despicable thing, that one human could bestow on another. But no, nothing has ever disgusted me more than seeing the debaucherous, and cruel way, you have treated this child."

Addressing the SAS officers in the doorway, he then said, "Excuse me gentlemen, but would you mind waiting in the hallway, and please close the door behind you."

"What wrong you?" said the General as Pedigrew kicked the door closed. "You Anglaise never have fun? Ha, your nation so boring." He nonchalantly laughed.

The sickly smell of Cordite intermingled with sulphuric smoke, shrouded the tiny room after Major Pedigrew Jennings released the trigger safety of his Browning pistol, before shooting General Yahmed through his blackened heart.

"Those who live by the sword – die by the sword!"

uttered Pedigrew, as he looked at the lifeless body of Yahmed. "I hope you rot in hell, you disgusting animal!"

Noticing the Generals Imbel Brazilian pistol, laying at the side of the filthy mattress, he bent over and firmly placed the gun in his left hand. His mind started to race as he thought of the abuse that Cathel's son must have endured, which so reminded him of similar circumstances he'd found himself in, after he'd once found a fellow operative who'd been tortured by Arab extremists and left for dead. He'd fastidiously visited the man throughout the following year at the mental institution where he'd been seconded, but alas, he never recovered from his inner mental anguish. Pedigrew had hated seeing his associates family, badly suffering, every time they gazed upon the broken shell of the man they had known and loved.

His wife committed suicide, six months later!!

Standing, he made his decision, and turning, shot the sobbing boy through the middle of his clammy forehead.

The sobbing instantly ceased, as the child fell to the floor!

He gazed down at the abused body of Patrick Charles Crumley and uncharacteristically was overcome with a cloud of sadness.

Suddenly he realised he still possessed the emotional ability to cry; long since hidden, deep down inside of his stoic demeanour.

He bent down to place the Taurus Brazilian pistol into the tensioning palm of Yahmed's hand, when the bedroom door flew open, and Cathel dashed into the room.

"Oh my God!" he remorsefully screamed, after noticing his loving son's tortured naked body, awkwardly lying in a pool of glistening blood, that was slowly seeping around his bereft of life, physical structure.

Instinctively, Cathel grabbed hold of the Major's taut

190

neck with both hands and squeezing as hard as humanly possible, went through the motions of 'unintentional' strangulation!

"You promised me! You promised me my son would be saved! You promised me he wouldn't be harmed and I trusted you! You lying conniving bastard, I hate you!"

Struggling to draw breath, the Major pressed Yahmed's pistol hard against Cathel's stomach and pulled the trigger!

Cathel sank to his knees; a look of complete bewilderment and surprise escaping from his sorrowful eyes, as he attempted to staunch the flow of blood trickling through his fingers by pressing the white golf shirt he was wearing, hard against the wound. The excruciating pain suddenly encapsulated his whole body!

Pedigrew knelt at his side. "I'm sorry old chap, but let's face it, nothing's fair in love and war. Tomorrow's newspapers around the world will have a photo of the body of you, Brendan Flynn, the famous movie star, and the body of your lovely, innocent young son, Patrick, lying beside you. Also in the photo, will be the body of General Melud Ali Yahmed of the Libyan Mukhabarat Secret Service, who was hired by the IRA to assassinate you both, who in turn was killed by SAS operatives."

He leaned towards Cathel who was noisily breathing in a haphazard manner. "Thanks to you Brendan, due to your celebrity status, which we created of course, the world will forever condemn the IRA for their vicious attack on you and your son. And it will totally destroy the idea that the IRA organisation is here to help the Catholics of this country, but instead, are using religion to create a dichotomy of the Irish people for their own ends, and thank goodness, all the money and support they receive from publicity shy donors will now cease."

He gently stroked Cathel's cheek who was now struggling with the intense pain from his wound. Pedigrew

191

could see it was now becoming unbearable.

He reiterated: "Brendan, the Provo's from now on, will be remembered as the brutal regime who killed an amazing famous actor, who will forever be praised, for saving the lives of so many British army personal, Regardless of his own life. And they will never forget his nine-year-old son who was brutally sodomised before his death. Also, the general populous of Northern Ireland and Europe will be disgusted to find out that the Provo's biggest benefactor is 'Mad Dog Gaddafi', who orders people killed for pleasure!! So you see, Cathel old chap, it was certainly money well spent, sending you to RADA. But of course that will be our secret!!"

He removed a Senior Service from his gold case and lit it. "Would you like a drag old boy?"

Cathel attempted to straighten up, but collapsed in agony. "Fuck you!" he managed to say through clenched teeth.

Pedigrew shook his head in pitiful annoyance and pressing the barrel of the Imbel pistol into Brendan's ear, said, "Goodbye old friend, I actually did like you." He pulled the trigger as he omitted a steady stream of cigarette smoke from his parched mouth.

Cathel slumped forward onto the cold floor.

Slithering across the linoleum floor on his knees, Pedigrew placed the pistol into General Yahmed's left hand, making sure to tightly wrap the General's fingers around the metal stock. Standing from his kneeling position, he gazed at the carnage strewn out in front of him.

"Excuse me sir," said Pedigrew's MI5 subordinate, who'd been stood quietly behind him throughout the messy ordeal. "I think you handled that situation rather well, if I may say so sir."

"Yes, I did, didn't I?" the major answered. "Now will you please send for the photographer, there's a good chap."